LOST IN AFRICA

Nick Warburton was a primary school teacher for ten years before deciding to become a full-time writer. He has written plays for stage, television and radio, including *Moonfleet* and *Conversations from the Engine Room*, which won the Radio Times Drama Award. For children, he has written *The Battle of Baked Bean Alley*; *Normal Nesbitt, The Abnormally Average Boy*; *To Trust a Soldier*; *Ackford's Monster*; *Dennis Dipp on Gilbert's Pond* and *Gladiators Never Blink*. A Visiting Fellow of University College, Chichester, Nick is married with a son and lives in Cambridge.

Books by the same author

Ackford's Monster
The Battle of Baked Bean Alley
Normal Nesbitt, The Abnormally Average Boy
To Trust a Soldier
You've Been Noodled!

LOST IN AFRICA

NICK WARBURTON

WALKER BOOKS
AND SUBSIDIARIES
LONDON • BOSTON • SYDNEY

First published 2000 by Walker Books Ltd
87 Vauxhall Walk, London SE11 5HJ

This edition published 2001

2 4 6 8 10 9 7 5 3 1

Text © 2000 Nick Warburton
Cover design © 2001 Walker Books Ltd

The right of Nick Warburton to be identified as author
of this work has been asserted by him in accordance
with the Copyright, Designs and Patents Act 1988.

This book has been typeset in Sabon

Printed in Great Britain by Cox & Wyman Ltd
Reading, Berkshire

British Library Cataloguing in Publication Data:
a catalogue record for this book is
available from the British Library.

ISBN 0-7445-7830-2

In memory of Wendy Boase

*With thanks to Peter and Susan Hilken
for their hospitality and advice*

Author's Note

Lost in Africa is set in West Africa but the places mentioned in the story – the towns and countries – are fictitious, as are the characters.

CHAPTER ONE
JANUARY 1972

I'm sitting under the canopy in the little steamer, with my feet resting on the crates, and I'm looking across the brown river to a line of dark trees at its edge. We're making steady progress, though it feels as if we're remaining still while the whole of Africa is chugging slowly by behind us.

"Goes on and on, doesn't it, Natasha?" the guide calls out to me.

He's sitting in the bows with a cloth draped over his head, and one knee bent, ready to kick the engine when it chokes.

"Do you recognize anything yet?" he says.

"No, not yet," I answer, "but I'll know it when I see it."

A clearing at the waterside. A little white house on stilts. Yes, I'll know it when I see it. It's more than ten years since I was last on this river, but my memory grows stronger with every mile we cover. Those brooding trees, the slow river, Colin and Alex. And my father. Most of all I remember Daddy.

CHAPTER TWO
DECEMBER 1961

I took my little brother to the ship's rail and pointed across the sea to a strip of green coast like a low cloud.

"Look, Colin," I said. "Africa. We'll see Daddy soon."

Colin always loved that first sighting because to him the Palm Coast was a place of secrets and excitement. It didn't seem like that to me. I just wanted to be back in England, sitting by Aunt Sylvia's coal fire with the rain running down the windows and my birthday cards on the mantelpiece. I looked across the sea and thought that it would be nice, just for once, to have a birthday in England. I had no say in the matter though. With a father like Ronnie Banham, you had no say in *any* matter. He was always telling me how lucky I was.

"Not many people have African birthdays, Natasha."

"Apart from Africans," I'd remind him.

"You know what I mean."

Once I tried to tell him. I suggested, quite politely, that I might have my birthday in England, just for a change, because, after all, England was my home.

"Nonsense, old girl," he said. "You were born in Africa."

"I was *supposed* to be born in England though. Mummy was supposed to come home and…"

"Yes, yes. But you were early. You took us all by surprise. You are English in a sense, of course, but you were born in the Palm Coast, so that's just as much home. Naturally so."

Naturally so.

So we stood by the rail, my little brother and I, breathing the humid air and waiting to dock in Liberation for the Christmas holidays. The bags in our cabin were stuffed with presents from Aunt Sylvia back in London, and propped against the wall was the set of golf clubs Daddy had asked us to bring. Soon we'd see him among the crowds on the harbour wall, red-faced, bossy, wearing shorts the size of a small tent.

"And we'll have our party when we see him, won't we, Natasha?" said Colin.

"Yes, we'll have our party."

The party was to be a three-way celebration – for our arrival in Africa, my birthday tucked in the middle somewhere and Daddy's promotion. After years of travelling all over the Palm Coast for the Service, he was to be given the job of running a museum in Liberation. His letters had been full of plans for this new enterprise. He was just the man for the job, he said. Lots of local crafts and stuff. Right up his street. Tom Barker, the District Commissioner, had to confirm the decision of course, but he was certain to agree. And then there'd be no more going up-country for Ronnie Banham. Great changes ahead, children, great changes.

I felt Colin tug at my sleeve.

"Will he get a new uniform?" he asked hopefully. "With long trousers?"

"We'll soon find out."

I wanted to see Daddy again, I really did, but I was jittery with nerves. I knew I had to tell him. It wouldn't be easy but I had to tell him.

I don't want to come out here next time, Daddy. I want to stay in England for Easter.

I was hoping that the excitement of the new job might soften him up a bit, but the closer we came to seeing him again, the harder it was to imagine him even listening, and the easier it was to imagine him hitting the roof. I began to wish I'd talked to Aunt Sylvia about it. She was the only person who could tell Daddy anything.

"Don't be silly, Ronnie," she'd have said.

13

"Of course Natasha must stay with me."

But it was too tricky to explain – I hardly understood it myself – so I hadn't said anything to Aunt Sylvia either.

It was dusk when we finally got ashore. There were huge bands of gold and orange in the sky, but not for long – dusk is always over so quickly in Africa – and by the time all our luggage had been piled up around us, darkness had fallen. There was no sign of Daddy. People were shouting and waving, their faces shining in the light of huge lamps swinging from poles. Colin squeezed my hand and looked up at me with frightened eyes.

"Where is he, Nat?"

"It's all right. He'll be here somewhere."

But you couldn't be sure with Daddy – he was so unpredictable. People kept dancing up to us with friendly offers of help, and I kept shaking my head and refusing politely.

"No, thank you. We're waiting for Mr Banham."

Some of them knew him.

"Ah, Banham Pa! Good man, good man. Be along soon."

I was just thinking that I ought to contact the Station, and wondering where I might find a phone, when we heard a hearty shout over by the harbour gates – "Colin! Natasha!" – and there he was, threading his way through the crowd and flapping his arms above his head.

"Greetings, sunshine," he said, ruffling Colin's hair.

He gave me a wink and a punch on the arm.

"Happy birthday, old girl," he said. "Got something for you back in the Jeep. Show you in a minute. I think you'll like it."

"Where were you?" I asked.

"The District Commissioner sent me up-country for a week. Last minute arrangement. Couldn't get a message to you."

"We didn't know what to do."

"I know, old girl, but no harm done. Anyway, I asked the Station to send Daniel along in one of the trucks. Haven't seen him, have you?"

"No."

"Well, he'll be around somewhere. Daniel won't let us down."

He gave us his slight smile. Daddy, like a lot of Brits on the Station, only had three basic expressions: the slight smile, the slight frown, and the complete blank. And they didn't always mean what you thought they meant.

There was the usual sea of boys bobbing their heads and elbowing each other for the right to carry our luggage. Daddy picked one and told him to take our bags up to the harbour gates.

"And mind those golf clubs," he shouted as

the boy tottered away. "They're very expensive!"

The boy was swallowed up in the throng and all we could see of him was Daddy's golf bag perched sideways on his head. Just as we reached the gates, a white truck screeched to a halt in a cloud of dust. Daniel hopped out, sweeping his cap off and bowing.

"Greetings, greetings!" he called. "And how is good old England?"

"As it always is, Daniel," Daddy answered for us. "Drab. Isn't it, Natasha?"

Daniel chortled. England drab? No, no. How could that be when Her Majesty the Queen lives there and there are Christmas lights and soldiers with red uniforms and black and white cows and football teams all with the same colour shirts and…

Daniel had a vivid picture of England in his head, and loved to paint it for whoever would listen. He turned to me and bowed again.

"Little Ma," he said solemnly. "Welcome back."

That was what they called me at the Station after Mummy died – Little Ma. I smiled at him – it was hard not to smile when Daniel was around. Colin, half hidden by Daddy, reached out and took Daniel's hand.

"Oh my, oh my!" said Daniel. "Who's this chief? And where is Master Colin. You left him behind, Little Ma?"

"No, it's me, Daniel," Colin said. "I've just grown."

"Oh, yes. Soon be big and tall like Pa."

Daddy left Daniel to load our luggage and wandered across the road to where he'd parked his Jeep. He came back with a brown paper bag which he tossed to me.

"Here we are," he said. "Happy birthday, Natasha."

I opened it and my heart sank. It was a toy monkey. I looked up, hoping he was joking. He wasn't.

"Sweet little chap, isn't he? Thought he was just the thing."

I made myself smile at him and mutter thanks.

If he thinks I still like fluffy toys, I said to myself, he's in for a shock, and I tried again to picture how he'd take my news.

The thing is, Daddy ... I've been thinking, you see ... and maybe I should stay in England next Easter ... because, because...

Because what? Because, really, I was sick of Africa, of life on the Station – sitting around on verandas, sipping tea and exchanging chit-chat. That was what they expected of wives and daughters; they had to be refined and decorative, and I didn't want to be refined and decorative. I wanted to be useful. I couldn't say that without hurting him though. The Station was everything to him, it was his whole life.

CHAPTER THREE

Colin wanted to go with Daddy in his battered old Jeep, so I rode back with Daniel in the truck. I sat beside him, watching the headlights bumping over the red dirt and piercing the thick shadows under the palms.

"You are well, Little Ma?" he said after a while.

"Very well, Daniel. How are things at the Station?"

He wrenched the wheel to avoid a dog and we heard Daddy hoot his horn behind us. Daniel leaned out of the window and shouted over his shoulder.

"Sorry, Pa. Mad dog on road!"

Then he looked sideways at me.

"Things are dandy at the Station," he said. "Oh yes. Pretty dandy..."

But something in the way he said it made me think that perhaps it wasn't as dandy as it might've been.

"How's Joseph?" I asked. "Has he been keeping busy?"

Joseph was building Daddy's golf course. He was our house boy and had a room in the bungalow. The last time we were on the Station, Daddy told him to clear a patch of scrub and drill some holes at various points that he'd marked with piles of white stones.

"You planting trees, Pa?" Joseph asked.

"No, Joseph, not trees. I don't want anything in the holes."

"Just empty holes, Pa?"

"Just empty holes," said Daddy, and he produced a golf ball from his tunic pocket and held it up. "Fact is, I've decided to take up golf, so I need holes to hit the ball into. You see?"

"Certainly, Pa."

But I could tell he thought it was a mad idea – knocking a ball into little holes – and he kept finding excuses not to get on with it, so the golf course was still unfinished when Colin and I went back to England.

Daniel swerved round a pothole and muttered under his breath. Then he bounced a little in his seat, looking awkward and uncertain.

"How's Joseph?" I asked again. "Has he finished the golf course?"

"Yes. Nine holes with little flags," he said, adding in the same breath, "but Joseph has gone."

"Gone? Gone where?"

I was shocked to hear this. I couldn't imagine life on the Station without Joseph. I watched a black beetle smash into the windscreen and wriggle itself off again, and a sudden cold thought struck me.

"He isn't—" I began, "I mean, he wasn't ill or anything?"

"No, no, Ma. Joseph fit and well. Just gone. Back to his village."

"Does Daddy know?"

"No, no. I tell him pretty soon."

"But why did he leave?"

"Joseph say he want to be a farmer. To dig holes and *plant* things in them. Just now he take his pay and go."

Just like that. With no farewell or thought about Banham Pa and his family – the family he was part of, really.

"Barker Pa angry, though," Daniel went on. "Angry when Joseph left, and angry after. Still angry when I come to meet you. Being Top Man hard for Barker Pa. Decisions, decisions."

"What decisions?"

"Oh, things, different things. You know the Station, Little Ma. Lots of talk, not much sense. Maybe just angry and no reason."

He drove on into the night, with both hands firmly on the wheel and, for most of the time, his mouth firmly shut. I guessed he was fretting about whatever it was that made the District Commissioner angry.

When we swung up the drive into the Station, the headlights caught the edge of the graveyard, so I had a fleeting glance of the place where Mummy was buried. Not the headstone, but the three palms that leaned over it. Coming across it like that, suddenly and unexpectedly, caught me by the throat and I wanted to cry.

Banhams don't cry though. Neither the male nor the female of the species, Daddy always said. And they don't cry because they know it won't get them anywhere.

Although I couldn't see the headstone, I could picture it very clearly. A neat little grave where we put African flowers from time to time. African flowers weren't really right for Mummy – they were always too big and bright. I wanted to bring her primroses from England, but whenever I tried they wilted before we reached the Bay of Biscay.

Daddy jumped out of the Jeep, and came striding up to the truck to check on the golf clubs, and that was the moment Daniel chose to tell him about Joseph. He couldn't really have left it any longer or Daddy would've been up the path to the bungalow and discovered for himself.

For a second or two he was speechless with shock. Then he snapped at Daniel and asked him why he hadn't mentioned this before.

"Sorry, Pa," said Daniel. "Forgot."

"No, Daniel. Not forgot – didn't want to."

"My head spin round and I forgot, Pa."

Daddy muttered irritably to himself and began to haul his golf clubs out of the truck. There were lights in the next bungalow. Mrs Sneeth was sitting on her veranda reading a newspaper. (George Sneeth must've been away or she would've been talking to him. Mrs Sneeth was a great talker, while George only ever managed to speak in short sentences, like someone reading a telegram.)

The sounds of the clubs being dumped on the ground brought Mrs Sneeth to the veranda rail. She half raised her hand to wave, but she must've guessed that something was up because she lowered it again, folded her paper and went inside.

"After all I taught Joseph," Daddy muttered to himself. "I find that unforgivable. I go up-country for a week and he bally well *deserts* me. Because that's what it is: *desertion*."

He marched up the path to the bungalow, leaving Daniel and me to struggle after him with the rest of the cases and Colin.

"Good job Joseph not here," Daniel mumbled, half to me and half to himself. "He be in very hot water then."

"If he was here," I pointed out, "Banham Pa wouldn't be cross, would he?"

Daniel gave me a look that said he thought Banham Pa might be cross anyway – these days everyone seemed to be cross about something.

"What's the matter with Daddy?" Colin asked, trailing after us. "Why isn't Joseph here?"

A voice boomed at us from the darkness ahead.

"Will you stop gossiping back there?"

We hurried up the path and saw Daddy standing on the veranda. Someone had lit an oil lamp and hung it from a beam – a sort of welcome, I suppose – and its gentle glow made a silhouette of him. He'd propped his golf bag against the rail and was standing in front of the bungalow with his hands on his hips like some kind of lion-tamer.

"There's a hundred things to do and no house boy," he barked. "Gossiping will not help."

Then he turned on his heel, tripped over something on the veranda and went down with a thud and a curse. Daniel dropped his cases and sprinted after him. He leapt up the veranda steps in one stride.

"Pa, Pa! Everything all right?"

"What the dickens…" Daddy mumbled, groping about on his hands and knees.

"Oh, Pa, something else I forgot to tell," said Daniel, hovering over him. "Alexander has come to sit at your door."

"Who? What are you burbling about, man?"

"Alexander. Come in from Nabala. Been waiting for you…"

Then there was another voice – "Please, Pa. Sorry, Pa…" – and I saw a thin African sitting in the doorway and cradling his foot.

"This Alexander, Pa," Daniel said in a trembly voice. "Been waiting here two days for you come back."

"Hello, Banner Pa," said the thin African cheerfully. "Much greetings."

Daddy supervised the stashing of our luggage in the bedrooms and Alexander on one of the chairs at the dining table.

"Sit there," he ordered, "and don't move."

He tossed Daniel some matches and told him to light the oil lamps, and soon the room was filled with soft yellow light. Then he stood over Alexander, a golf club resting in the crook of his arm, and the slight frown on his face. I could see now that Alexander wasn't very old – maybe not much older than me. He sat with his hands on a bundle of papers balanced on his knees. He had high cheek bones and large eyes which he kept fixed on the rush matting.

"Now," said Daddy. "Who are you, and

what do you mean by tripping me up on my own doorstep?"

"Alexander," he answered, still looking at the floor. "Not mean to trip up, Banner Pa."

"Banham, *Banham*. What's this here?"

He tapped the bundle of papers with the club. Alexander lifted his head and smiled broadly.

"This my book, Banner Pa," he said.

Boys like Alexander often turned up at the Station looking for work with their 'books'. They were mostly letters from people they'd worked for, not really books at all, although everyone called them books. Sometimes they didn't tell you very much: a scrap of paper with items to buy from the market, or a note from some District Officer up-country to say this is an honest boy but it's not safe to eat his chicken stew.

Daddy was in no mood to look at Alexander's book.

"You hang about my door and trip me up," he said, "and you expect me to give you work?"

"Need house boy now, Pa."

"That's as maybe, but do I need *you*?"

I think Daddy was about to send him off with a flea in his ear, but he didn't get the chance because there was a tap at the door and the District Commissioner appeared, leaning casually against the frame.

Tom Barker was almost fifty, but good-looking in a leathery kind of way, with a little clipped moustache like one of those old English film stars. He was a reasonable, unflustered man – it was hard to imagine him being cross.

"Welcome back, Ronnie," he said softly, as if Daddy had just wandered round the corner to buy a paper. "Season's greetings, Natasha. Good trip?"

He didn't wait for an answer, but fixed his eyes on Daddy and asked if he might have a word.

"Of course, Tom," Daddy said. "Come in, come in."

"In the office, if you don't mind."

Daddy darted a quick glance at him and Mr Barker pulled an embarrassed face and looked at the toe of his boot.

"Come over in ten minutes or so, will you Ronnie?" he said. "When you've sorted things out a bit."

"If it's that urgent I'll come now."

I knew it rattled Daddy to be asked to talk business on his first night back after a trip up-country. Without even looking back at us, he told Daniel to keep an eye on Alexander, and me to keep an eye on Colin, then out he marched, almost pushing past Tom Barker.

CHAPTER FOUR

"You in charge now, Little Ma," Daniel said.

He turned to Alexander and told him to stay there, like a good fellow, and Alexander nodded – he had no intention of going anywhere. There was hardly any food in the bungalow. I thought about going out to borrow some. Mrs Sneeth would've given us something, but I couldn't face her probing questions.

"How's the homeland, Natasha? And how is dear Ronnie after his trip? Is there something the matter? I couldn't help noticing…"

So I rooted around in our bags and found some biscuits, and a tin of beans on a shelf which I opened and gave to Colin cold. Then I went back to the dining room. Daniel was sitting at the table looking at Alexander who was leafing through the papers in his book. I asked him if he'd been a house boy before, which was a mistake, as things turned out, but I couldn't stand the heavy silence.

"No, Ma," said Alexander, "but I been small boy some time."

A small boy worked for a house boy – rather like a butler and his footman. We never had a small boy, though. It wasn't necessary because Joseph had been so efficient. He did everything in the house.

"Where were you when you were small boy?" I asked.

"Nabala, Ma. Small boy up there at resting station when Niff Pa come see."

"Niff Pa?"

"He mean Sneeth Pa," Daniel explained. "His names not good."

Alexander sifted through his book, brought out a piece of limp yellow paper and held it up to me. It was a note from George Sneeth – short and to the point – just the way he spoke.

Three days at Nabala. Alexander helped the house boy while I was there. He did his work well, as far as it's possible to judge. G. Sneeth.

When I looked up at Alexander, he was smiling at me.

"You see? I make good house boy."

"Why did you leave Nabala?" I said.

"Fighting, Ma. Soldiers come to my village. From over the border. From Tumani."

"Was it bad?"

"My father killed; my brothers killed," he

said simply. "My mother and my sisters run away, so I come down here. Safe here. People friendly."

And he smiled. He looked so untroubled. All the terrible things that must've happened to him and he was just smiling and hoping.

So I said he could be our house boy.

As soon as I said it I knew Daddy would be furious. I had to do *something*, though. I couldn't just pack Alexander off and tell him "bad luck but it's nothing to do with us". And, anyway, we did *need* a house boy. I told myself Daddy would come round to the idea eventually, but I didn't really believe it.

I got Colin ready for bed and waited for Daddy to return. Daniel disappeared. I didn't see him go – he was just there one moment and gone the next. I think he guessed there was more trouble in the wind, and he'd seen enough of an angry Banham Pa for one day. Alexander bustled about as happy as Larry, unpacking bags and putting chairs straight. Daddy wouldn't like that either – his things mauled about by a strange boy. I was tucking the mosquito net round Colin's bed when I heard boots on the path outside and froze.

"What's the matter, Nat?"

"It's all right," I said. "I just heard Daddy come in."

"Tell him to come and say good night."

"Yes. Yes, of course."

29

I took a deep breath and went straight to the kitchen where Alexander was arranging tins on a shelf and singing softly to himself. I told him to stay there and make no sound because Banham Pa was tired and didn't want to be disturbed. Then I pushed the door into the dining room.

"Daddy," I said as I went in. "There's something I have to tell you."

He sat at the table looking at both hands spread out in front of him.

"What is it?" he said quietly.

"About the boy. You know, the boy on the veranda?"

"Who?"

"The one you tripped over…"

"Oh, him," he said, and then he breathed in through his nose and straightened himself up in his chair. "Listen, Natasha, my dear. Forget the boy for a moment. I have something to tell *you*."

And that's when I knew for certain that something was wrong. He hardly ever called me "my dear". I sat opposite him and held my breath.

"Barker wanted to talk to me about the museum."

"Why? It's still going ahead, isn't it?"

"Oh, yes. It's going ahead. But without me. I haven't got the job, Natasha. I've been overlooked."

I was stunned. He'd been so sure of this new job, so happy about it. He sat there looking worn out and shocked, like someone who'd just been dragged out of a brawl.

"George is going to run it," he said flatly. "George Sneeth."

"But he hasn't been in the Service as long as you."

"No. They consider him the better man, I suppose."

"Why?"

"I don't know…"

"But Daddy, I thought Mr Barker had promised you…"

"He had. Not in writing of course, but he told me. He said he couldn't see any problems with me getting the post. And now he's changed his mind."

"Didn't he give you any reasons?"

"Nothing that made any sense. He said there was still valuable work for me to do up-country. Then he said I was too abrasive."

"What did he mean by that?"

"That I argue too much, I suppose. Which is utter nonsense, Natasha, isn't it? I get on with people as well as anyone I know," he said, heaving a sigh. "No, Natasha, there's only one way of looking at it: I've been snubbed."

He sighed again and Alexander walked steadily out of the kitchen, his gaze fixed on two cups of tea on a small tray.

"What's this?" asked Daddy, narrowing his eyes at him.

"Tea, Banner Pa. Good for tiredness."

"Who told him he could make tea?"

"I'm afraid I did, Daddy. I thought with Joseph gone and everything…"

"What?"

"Well … without a house boy … and Colin to look after…"

"He's our new house boy?"

I swallowed and nodded, waiting for the explosion. Alexander set the cups delicately in front of us and backed out, grinning.

"I see…" Daddy said absently. "Yes. Good idea. What's his name again?"

"Alexander."

"Alexander … right. Well done, Natasha."

And he picked up his cup and sipped his tea. So there was no hitting of roofs, no explosions. Alexander was now our house boy, appointed by me and officially accepted by Daddy, who had more important things to worry about than who was going to make the tea.

Daddy said that losing the museum job was a "setback". It was his word for whatever went wrong. Spilling the milk, losing a sock, getting your leg wrenched off by a gorilla – they were all setbacks.

"But I can tell you now, Natasha," he said,

"I shan't take this lying down. That is not the Banham way."

He meant it wasn't *his* way. Aunt Sylvia would've given a little sigh and carried on – and she's a Banham. "Oh well," she'd say, "these things are sent to try us, I suppose. Now don't make a fuss, Ronnie. Press on, press on."

"Justice has not been done," he said. "And it *must* be done."

"What're you going to do?" I asked timidly.

"Do?" he said. "I've already done it."

For one horrible moment I thought he'd punched Mr Barker on the nose. I suddenly pictured him crumpled in a corner, trying to stop the bleeding with a wet cloth. It wasn't that, though.

"I have resigned," he said shortly. "Resigned on the spot."

And I thought: we're going back to England. It was mean of me, I expect, but that was the first thing that came into my head. He's resigned and we're going home. I won't ever have to tell him about my plans. Saved at the last moment.

Then I remembered that he'd resigned before – over one thing or another that upset him – and he'd always changed his mind, or been talked out of it.

He gave me a sidelong glance.

"I know what you're thinking," he said.

"This time I really mean it though. I have finished with the Service. From tonight I am a free man."

CHAPTER FIVE

Mr Barker came round in the morning and Daddy greeted him like a long lost friend.

"Tom! Come in and have some of Alexander's splendid tea. Have you met Alexander, by the way? He's our new house boy."

They disappeared into the dining room and I loitered around on the veranda. Five minutes later the joviality had gone and they were shouting at each other. Or rather, Daddy was shouting. All I could hear from Mr Barker was a sort of steady, reasonable grumbling. Then out they came, briskly swinging their arms, like men in a walking race, Daddy wearing his slight smile and Mr Barker looking pale and anxious.

"Do call again, Tom," Daddy called after him as he strode down the path. "But only if you've changed your mind!"

Then he dropped into the wicker chair, arms

folded and grinning to himself, and he was still there just before lunch when Mrs Sneeth turned up.

"Gloria!" he said, springing up. "Lovely to see you! Sorry we didn't catch you last night. We were a little late arriving, and then, of course, I had to tender my resignation."

"Yes," she said darkly. "I heard. Do you really think, Ronnie…?"

"I do, I do," he said.

He was trying to be jolly and dignified at the same time, like some kind of Father Christmas in huge shorts, but it wasn't convincing.

"Come in, Gloria," he went on. "Alexander's been frying up some bananas. We'll see how he's managed, shall we?"

And off *they* went into the dining room. Then it was the same routine – mumbled conversation followed by shouting from Daddy and high-pitched wailing from Mrs Sneeth.

"But Ronnie, think of the girl, and Colin…"

"The girl," she called me. That was typical of the Station – I wasn't important enough to have a name.

"That is precisely *why* I'm doing this, Gloria. I have my pride, you know."

And out he came, same brisk walk and slight smile, practically steering Mrs Sneeth down the steps. Her mouth was twisted, as if she were going to cry, or spit. Both, probably.

So, by lunchtime, I knew he'd made up his

mind and would stick to his guns. Stick to your guns – that was the Banham way. I was sorry for him, of course, but I couldn't help feeling light-hearted at the same time.

We'll be going home, I kept thinking. To England. *Home to England.*

I woke up next morning to the sounds of a terrible row outside my window – shouting and banging and boxes being thrown about. I looked out and saw the door of the small shed standing open. We used it to store the stuff we didn't need every day, so I could hardly remember the last time the door stood open. A tumble of old boxes and crates had spilled out of it – the start of our packing, I assumed – and Daddy and Alexander were jumping around and thrashing the long grass with canes. There was nothing unusual about that: I guessed they must've disturbed a snake or something. By the time I got outside, the panic was over and they were busying themselves with the boxes.

"Put this lot over there," Daddy told Alexander. "And put these here. This pile I do want, and that pile I don't."

"Understand, Banner Pa. Right-oh."

Daddy held up a cardboard box for him to see, and then threw it aside, pulling a disgusted face to show what he meant. The box was soggy from being in the shed so long and when it thudded to the ground it split and a few old

Beanos fanned out in the grass.

"*Don't want*," he said slowly.

I hadn't read the *Beano* for years, but seeing them tossed aside as rubbish made me want to rescue them. Daddy had already moved on though. He took up a small wooden crate and held it up for Alexander's benefit.

"*Do want*," he said and switched on his slight smile.

He put the crate gently down at his feet.

"Understand, Alexander? *Do want* in a neat pile here; *don't want* in a heap over there."

"Yes, sah," said Alexander as if it was all suddenly clear, though I had the feeling that he'd known what Daddy had meant from the outset.

"Ah, Natasha," said Daddy when he noticed me. "You can lend a hand. We're sorting things to take with us."

"We are leaving, then?" I said.

"Of course we're leaving, girl. I'm a man of my word, you ought to know that by now. And I've had just about all the nonsense I can take from the likes of Barker."

There was a plaintive cry from the bungalow: Colin waking up and finding himself on his own.

"Go and see to the little chap, Alexander," said Daddy. "Feed and water him, will you? And don't say anything about leaving. Not just yet."

Alexander gave a short bow and hurried indoors. We watched him for a moment. He seemed completely at ease after such a short time with us, almost as if Joseph had left his spirit behind and he'd slipped it on, like an old coat.

"You haven't told Colin about us leaving, have you?" Daddy asked me suddenly.

"How could I? You've only just told me."

"Rubbish. I remember telling you. And anyway, what did you think? That I could resign and stay here? We *have* to leave. Just don't mention it to Colin. It'll only set him off asking awkward questions."

He turned on his heel and disappeared into the shed. An old lamp-shade came flying out – "*Don't want* pile, please, Natasha!" – and then he gave a cry of triumph and backed out again, lugging Colin's old pram behind him. He wrenched it from side to side, biffing boxes out of the way.

"I knew it," he said. "I knew we still had this old thing."

He gave it a shove and it rolled creakily towards me. I caught hold of it and directed it towards his *don't want* pile.

"What are you doing? What are you doing?" he snapped.

"Well, we won't want this, will we?" I said.

"Of course we will. This is what I've been looking for for the last half hour."

"But Daddy, why do we want a pram? We'll have to get it on the ship and…"

"Ship? What are you talking about, ship? We're not going on a ship, old girl."

"You mean we're flying?"

"With a pram? Use your loaf. No, we're walking. So obviously we'll need a pram to put our things in. Unless you want to carry them."

I stood there staring at him and trying to make sense of what he'd just said. Walking? *Where* were we walking?

"I don't understand," I said.

"Oh, Natasha, it's perfectly simple. I have resigned so we have to leave."

"You mean … on foot?"

"Well, that's how people usually walk, isn't it?"

"But … but where are we going? Aren't we going home?"

"Africa is our home, Natasha. They don't want us here so we must go somewhere else, somewhere far from the Station. It's no good going south – we'll end up in the sea – and we can't go north or east, so obviously, we must follow the coast road. South-east. Now bring that pram back to the *do want* pile."

That night I dreamed I was running round and round Aunt Sylvia's garden in the splashing rain. Then I woke up and realized I was still in Africa, and I thought, this is stupid. *Walking*?

We can't possibly walk! Because it wouldn't be like walking in England – neat paths and signposts, and somewhere to buy lemonade. It didn't make sense to walk in Africa. Anyway, there was no *need* to walk. Mr Barker could give us travel documents. The Service had trucks and things that went all over the place – right up to the border, if you were mad enough to want to go that way. He could contact resting stations between Liberation and almost anywhere else in West Africa, and make sure there'd be someone to meet us.

Daddy would have none of this.

"I'm not asking that buffoon Barker for anything," he said. "I want no help, Natasha. We are walking so you might as well get used to the idea. I have my pride."

So all through the day he sorted out his stupid *don't want* pile and his ridiculous *do want* pile. They started out about the same size – two great mountains of irregular-shaped rubbish with bits of our past sticking out of them. There were the *Beanos*, and the smelly old canvas bath Daddy took on his trips up-country, and an old blanket I remembered from the time I was ill with a fever, all sorts of things. Some of it I could hardly bear to look at.

There was a mirror in a cane frame with two little wicker drawers which used to stand by Mummy's bed. I saw him haul it out of the shed and stand there thinking about it. He stood for two or three minutes, deep in thought, and then balanced it carefully on the *do want* pile.

It was obvious we'd never manage all those things though, and later in the day he started to fling stuff across from one pile to the other. Just before darkness fell, I went to see how he was getting on, and he'd managed to reduce the *do want* pile till it was small enough to fit into Colin's old pram and a couple of rucksacks. The mirror was nowhere to be seen.

He was staring intently at the loaded pram like an artist studying his latest work. I'd never seen him so still and unruffled before. I suppose he'd tired himself out. He heard me approach and half turned.

"You see, Natasha," he said. "This stands for my life in the Palm Coast. Not very much, is it?"

I was still feeling crotchety and didn't answer. My dream of going home had been dumped on the *don't want* pile with everything else, and I thought, of course it's not very much; you've just thrown about three tons of it out.

He had a fat book under his arm and he put it carefully on top of the pram, like an old soldier laying a wreath on a war memorial.

"There'll be plenty of time for reading on our journey," he said. "I've read it before, of course, but I shall look forward to reading it again."

"What is it?" I asked.

He picked it up again and showed me. It was *War and Peace*. It had a grubby red cloth cover and it smelled like an old sack.

"I read it on a couple of trips up-country. Did I ever tell you?"

"No."

"I thought I did. I finished it the night after you were born. That's why you were called Natasha, you know. After the girl in the story."

Alexander came out with Colin in tow. Each had a small tray with tall glasses of lemonade on them and Colin was walking cautiously, putting one little foot in front of the other and keeping his eyes on the tray. I suddenly felt so sorry for him.

"Thirsty work, Banner Pa," smiled Alexander.

(Daddy had given up trying to persuade him to get the name right by this time.)

"You've been most helpful, Alexander," he said as he took the drink. "Most helpful. I shall write something nice in your book."

Alexander stopped smiling.

"But, sah, not need my book. I work for you…"

"But don't you realize? We're leaving here. Tomorrow we shall be gone."

"Yes, Banner Pa, I know. But I come too.

43

Most certainly."

"You can't."

Alexander blinked at him.

"I'm sorry, Alexander. I don't work for the Service now. But I shall see that you have a job with someone. Perhaps Mrs Sneeth will be wanting…"

"No, sah. I am useful boy, useful on journey…"

"You don't understand…"

He would've spelled it out for him – all the reasons why it was impossible to take a house boy where we were going – but I couldn't bear it any longer, so I cut in.

"Please, Daddy."

"What?"

"He wants to stay with us."

And instead of barking at me, Daddy pursed his lips and nodded.

"All right," he said. "You come too, Alexander. Good man."

He slapped him on the shoulder and it was like switching on a light. The smile came back. Then Colin tugged at Daddy's shorts.

"Why's my old pram here?" he asked.

"We're taking it for a walk, old man."

"All of us?"

"All of us. It'll be an adventure, Colin, old boy. You'll like it. But you'll have to be tough, too, because it might be a long walk."

The thought of a long walk didn't seem to

worry Colin. He felt inside his shirt and brought out my birthday monkey.

"Can we take Hubert with us?" he asked.

CHAPTER SIX

There were big shadows swinging over the walls of my bedroom and a globe of golden light somewhere. Someone was scrunching up the mosquito net and pulling it aside. It was Daddy with an oil lamp, his face hanging over me, half in sharp darkness and half in streaks of light.

"Natasha, get up," he was saying. "We're leaving."

"Now?" I mumbled. "But I've got to speak to Mrs Sneeth…"

"Don't be silly. We're not speaking to anyone. Now hurry up. We must leave before the sun comes up. I don't want anyone to know we've gone."

Colin and I sat together at the table, our heads propped on our hands, our eyes barely open, while Daddy bustled in and out with a strange meal of odds and ends, halfway between breakfast and tea. It was made up of just about everything he'd managed to find in the kitchen – dried fruit and nuts, some cake and biscuits and squares of jelly. He'd also gathered six or seven eggs and scrambled them in a large saucepan.

"Tuck in," he said. "Easiest way to carry food is on the inside."

"But we can't eat this. It's horrible…"

"An army marches on its stomach, Natasha."

"But eggs and jelly…"

"It doesn't matter what it is. And anyway, we can't be sure where our next meal will come from. Get on, and be quick about it."

Alexander came in, bright and cheerful, with some mugs of tea.

"Morning, Ma. We off today," he said and I raised my eyebrows at him and chewed on some cake.

Colin liked that mish-mash of a meal. He was licking his plate – a thing Mummy would never have let him do – when Daddy started to joggle the pram through the door and down the steps.

"Off we go. Off we go."

"But I haven't brushed my teeth," I heard myself say.

It sounded pathetic, and so young, and it made him stop in the doorway and turn round.

"That's civilization, my girl," he snorted.

47

"We're leaving all that behind."

"But you have to clean your teeth…"

"No time, no time. You can chew on a twig. Much better than toothpaste."

He was in no mood to listen to protests, so I took Colin by the hand and we trundled outside where Daddy was manoeuvring the pram up the path without a backward glance at his old home. I had never really liked it, but it had been at least a home of sorts, and I didn't know if we'd ever see another one, so I stopped and took one last look at it. All I could see through the open door were our plates and mugs in a circle of light under the oil lamp on the table, and Alexander leaning over it with his hand cupped. He blew into the funnel and the path and the bungalow were instantly lost in darkness.

It wasn't easy, walking in the dark, and several times we wandered off the track and had to double back. But I don't think Daddy minded that: it was a problem to solve. Eventually the sun jumped up and we trudged along the coastal road, mostly in silence. When Colin dragged behind and grizzled, Daddy hoisted him up and gave him a piggyback. Alexander offered to help but Daddy wouldn't hear of it. This was his idea, and Colin was his son, so he would do the carrying. And if Colin got tired and hung from his neck till he nearly choked him, well, so much the better. Another little problem to solve.

When we were well clear of the Station, we stopped for a breather and boiled a pan of water over a little fire. We huddled round it, all four of us, hugging our knees and watching the sun shimmering over the sea.

"Banner Pa?" Alexander said after a while. "I think there is village along road."

"There is. So what?"

"Maybe we stop there, sah?"

"We can't be forever stopping, Alexander."

"We stop at village, they have water maybe."

"I don't know…"

"Daddy," I said. "We've only stopped once so far…"

"I know, Natasha, but I'll feel easier when we've crossed the river. Barker will have the devil of a job to follow us after that."

"Perhaps he won't follow us at all."

"He'll follow, old girl. He won't like the thought of someone walking off his Station. And I don't want to give him the satisfaction…"

"Colin tired, Banner Pa," Alexander said. "Two, three more hours, we need water. Village give us water. Help us many ways."

"How?"

"Help to cross river, Pa."

"Look, Alexander, you are the house boy. Don't keep offering me advice…"

"But he's right, Daddy. We can't get over the river without a boat, and if they let us use one in the village…"

He looked sharply at me, but he could see that we were talking sense – we would need a boat, and the water would run out soon.

"Well," he muttered. "We'll see."

Before we set off again, Alexander kicked out the fire. Seeing the embers scattered and growing cool made me think of the little grate in Aunt Sylvia's front room, and I suddenly remembered it was Christmas Eve. I pictured snow on branches and the Christmas tree in the corner, and for a second the smell of our dying fire became the smell of pine needles. But, of course, we were walking away from all the places where Christmas meant anything.

Then Daddy lifted Colin on to Alexander's back – he didn't say a word about changing his mind – and we plodded on.

It took us over two hours to reach the village. It was small, on the edge of the mangrove swamp. We knew we were getting close to the swamp when the mosquitoes began to appear in abundance – darting little electric dots which speckled our hands and jigged in front of our eyes. Most of the time I walked with my head down, looking at the ground, but whenever I glanced up I could see Daddy's broad red neck and the patch of sweat on the back of his shirt, about twenty paces ahead of us, marching stiffly in a world of his own. He rounded a spiky-leaved bush and stopped still, his hand held up to stop us too. Just ahead were several children under a tree, and beyond them a collection of square huts.

The children were playing with a feather, skipping about and trying to keep it in the air by patting at it with their hands and crouching beneath it to blow it upwards. They were so intent on all this that they didn't notice us.

"Children!" Daddy called out, suddenly and loud. "Children!"

They turned to look at us and froze. The feather swooped to the ground at their feet. I expected them to be afraid – this tall white man with his big hat and his powerful voice – but they weren't. They grinned and came running up to him, shouting and laughing. He shook hands and ruffled hair, bellowing with laughter. In next to no time the whole village had gathered round us. They were all talking at once and a dozen little brown hens were clucking and darting under our feet.

"Where is motor, Banham Pa?" asked a tall man with grey curls. "How you get here without motor?"

"It's up the road, Baba," Daddy said with a smile. "Wanted to walk the last bit."

"Walk?" said Baba, and he lifted his head and laughed. "You Station people all crazy."

"Well, you see, we have to cross the river. Can't take the motor across the river, can I? Need a boat."

The old man tapped the side of the pram and his eyes twinkled.

"Ah. This your boat?"

"This is our pram. With things to carry over the river. So the boat must be big enough to take it. Got a boat like that, have you, Baba?"

"Maybe, maybe. You come in first. Tell me about children. First time you bring children, Banham Pa. You tell me about them."

And certainly they were interested in us. Or rather, they were interested in Colin. They made a great deal of fuss of him, patting his cheek and running his hair through their fingers, and he loved it. They were polite to me – for Daddy's sake, I suppose – but I could see they weren't impressed. A girl-child? Oh, well, you had good fortune second time, Pa. A bit like the Station, really: somehow girls didn't count.

Baba led us into his hut. You could tell he was the chief because it was built with a few bricks and had a corrugated iron roof. The others were mostly mud. I could see handprints in the walls.

Daddy didn't tell them he'd walked out of his job. He let them think he was on important business on the other side of the river. He needed a boat to take four people and a pram.

Baba shook his head and said that such a thing could not be found, not anywhere, not at all, but Daddy unfolded some money, slowly, counting it note by note, and suddenly there was a boat that might just do, yes. Baba would see to it. Tomorrow.

CHAPTER SEVEN

When the sun came up we went down to the river, and Baba, with a proud gesture, showed us a canoe grounded on a mud bank. It was long and flat, hewn out of a single black log. There was a little more wrangling over the price, which seemed to have gone up overnight, so Daddy offered a little more and bought it outright.

"We only want to cross the river, Baba," he grumbled. "You'll send a man over in a day or two and bring it back to sell to some other mug."

"Mug, Banham Pa?" Baba said with a lift of his shoulders. "What is mug?"

He told some men to carry Colin, the rucksacks and the pram across the knee-deep mud. Daddy, Alexander and I waded out under our own steam. It took about ten minutes to get us all settled. It would've taken five if everyone hadn't tried to lend a hand. In the end though, we were sitting in the canoe like royalty, except that our legs were caked in grey sludge. Three men crouched at the back to shove us off, and Daddy stood up and waved his hat. The men heaved forward. Daddy wobbled and sat down. Then we were sliding over the mud and the front of the canoe was dipping into the brown water.

On the bank the villagers were waving back at us and shouting excitedly. But there was also another sound – a sort of whine that at first seemed to come from them, and then from the cloud of red dust billowing over the village behind them.

"Damn," muttered Daddy, squinting under his hand. "Damn and blast."

The crowd parted and I saw one of the Service trucks bumping down to the edge of the mud. A door flung open and a figure walked out of the cloud. It was Mr Barker.

"Ronnie," he called as he strode to the river edge. "Ronnie, what are you doing?"

"You can see what I'm doing, Tom. I'm going for a spin on the river."

"Don't be foolish, man…"

"I don't think there's anything left for us to say to each other, so if you don't mind…" Daddy said, stooping to pick up a paddle.

All the villagers stood perfectly still as the dust settled, and for a moment there was an eerie silence. Then the upper branches of a nearby tree rustled and about a dozen little grey parrots whirled away across the river. Colin lifted his head to follow their flight, but nobody else did.

"Don't do this, Ronnie," said Mr Barker. "Think about Natasha and Colin."

"I have thought about them, and that's exactly why I am doing this."

"I was driving around all yesterday looking for you," Mr Barker shouted with sudden impatience. "Let's talk about this. Let's see if we can work something out."

Daddy looked steadily at him and then turned his back. Mr Barker took off his helmet and wiped his brow.

"All right, Ronnie," he said quietly. "Maybe you've got a point, but why don't you let the children go?"

I felt my hands grip the sides of the canoe. Mr Barker swished at the mosquitoes in front of his face and looked directly at me.

"Natasha, I don't want to frighten you but this is not at all safe, you know. I'm sure Ronnie won't mind if you and Colin wanted to come back with me."

He softened his voice, trying to pretend that all this talk of leaving made perfect sense, that everything was absolutely all right. Daddy fixed his gaze up-river and said nothing, and I could tell that Mr Barker had touched a nerve.

There *were* dangers waiting for us. If I climbed out now, and took Colin with me, he wouldn't stop me.

"We'll take care of them, Ronnie. Just for a while, till we see you again…"

Then I heard myself speak, and I was saying thank you very much but I think I'll stay with Daddy. It was like hearing someone else – I hardly recognized my own voice. I was saying what I couldn't possibly mean, because going back was the obvious thing to do. We would be safe and Daddy would tramp around on his own until his mood passed and he came back to us. But I said we'd be all right, as if I were politely turning down another cup of tea or something.

"Thank you very much, but we'll be all right."

The canoe was already half in the water, and two firm strokes from Daddy's paddle slid us out on to the creamy brown river.

"Ronnie! Come back here!" Mr Barker shouted, raising both fists in the air and darting towards the mud.

"Farewell, Barker, old man, and happy Christmas!"

In no time we were well out on the river and pulling steadily away and the figures on the bank grew smaller and sounded fainter by the minute. We rounded a clump of mangroves and they were lost to sight. The last we heard was Mr Barker's voice shouting after us.

"I'm not leaving this, Ronnie! I'm going to fetch more men and we'll bring you back! Do you hear? I'm going to bring you back!"

The river was nothing like the tidy rivers of England. It was really a slow brown lake with clumps of mangroves on it, like islands, and you couldn't tell whether they were growing on mud banks or straight up out of the water. Neither could you tell which was the main river because so many channels ran between the mangrove clumps. Some meandered away to dead-ends.

"Where we go, Banner Pa?" said Alexander. He and Daddy had been paddling for some hours.

"Up river as far as we can," Daddy answered. "Then we'll cross to the other side. They'll have a job to find us there."

"Then best thing, stay in middle. Good and wide."

"No, no, I think not, Alexander. I've seen the maps and this river travels in a wide curve. We can cut some corners through the mangroves..."

"Not go through mangroves, Pa. Not good way..."

"Don't dispute with me, boy. I've seen the maps. I have a picture in my head and I know what I'm doing."

58

So Alexander held his tongue and we headed down one of the channels into a tunnel of gloom. All around us the branches and roots of the mangroves reached into the water like the thin fingers of a giant. You couldn't tell which was root and which was branch. A foot or two below the high tide mark they were crusty and pale, like bones. Above that they coiled up to a dark green canopy blotched with sunlight. The further in we moved, the more those fingers seemed to gather around us, and we were surrounded by a stench of mud and decay.

"Not quick now," said Alexander, not quite to himself.

"What was that?"

"We move not so quick now."

"Because you don't understand, Alexander. I've seen the map and it says we can cut off this corner of the river. I know what I'm doing."

But almost as soon as he said this, the front of the canoe lodged between two snaking roots and stuck, as if the fingers had pinched together and held us.

"Paddle back, paddle back."

They began to work the paddles in the other direction, but the canoe was wedged tight and Alexander had to lean out and force the roots apart to release us. When the canoe broke free, we skimmed suddenly backwards and Alexander was strung like a bridge between us and the mangrove roots.

"Stop arsing around, boy. We're wasting time."

I held on to Alexander's legs and he clambered back in, breathing hard and grinning with relief.

"Now," said Daddy, "we just back-paddle until we're clear again."

They dug the paddles in, the canoe shot back a few yards and thumped into more roots.

"Look," said Colin. "The trees have grown."

"Nonsense, Colin. We haven't been here that long."

The mangroves hadn't grown, of course, but bit by bit the water level had been slipping down. It must've fallen a couple of feet because there were now many more tangles of white root showing. So many, in fact, that we were caged in by them.

"Oh, this is *ridiculous*. We got in so we can get out."

But we sat there, unable to move, for what seemed hours in the rotting prison of those white tendrils, stench and silence all around us. The only sound came from an occasional flight of parrots breaking out overhead. So we lounged, and flapped at the mosquitoes, and waited, because waiting was all we could do. Only when the bottom of the canoe scraped against some submerged coils did we know for certain that the tide was still going out. Daddy told us all to sit still but sitting still didn't help. Minute by minute one end of the canoe lifted and we were tilted out. We clung to the mangroves to prevent ourselves from being pitched into the river. Alexander busied himself with some rope, making a noose to fix to the pram so that it didn't slip into the water.

Half an hour later, the nose of the canoe was at such a crazy angle that we were half sitting in it and half perching on the slimy roots. Then the tide turned and water began to flow back up the river, though it was too sluggish to see much difference.

"Ah," said Daddy, when the canoe righted itself at last. "That's more like it. Soon be out of here now."

We dozed and waited a little longer. Colin took his boots and socks off and dangled his legs over the side. I sat staring at bits of logs floating by. Strange, grey-green logs that seemed to move with a will of their own. Pushed along by the tide, I thought. One came close, heading for Colin's feet and I felt a flush of cold blood wash through me as I realized what it was.

Not a log – a crocodile.

I think I screamed – not for help: there wasn't time to scream for help. At the same time I grabbed Colin by the shirt and yanked him back. He tumbled backwards into the canoe, his head drummed against the bottom, and he wailed with shock and pain. Alexander saw the crocodile seconds after I had. He grabbed the paddle and took a swing at its snout, but the crocodile had already gone. All he managed to do was rock the canoe and shower us with swamp water.

"Don't you listen to a thing I say?" Daddy barked. "Never, *never* dip your feet over the side."

I don't know how much time we lost in there – most of the day, I suppose – but it didn't really matter. We didn't have anywhere special to go, so who cared how long it took? Then, as we came out under clear blue sky again, Alexander stopped paddling and knelt up, alert and listening. Daddy was still working away with his paddle at the back of the canoe, so we found ourselves turning a slow circle.

"What are you doing, boy? Keep at it, keep at it!"

"Listen, Pa. Voices."

And sure enough, thin voices could be heard far away to our left. There was nothing to be seen – only the broad river and the clumps of mangroves – but the voices were plain enough, coming like little stones skimming over the brown water.

"Barker," muttered Daddy. "Blast him."

So back into our cage of roots and branches we went, keeping low and watching the river through a curtain of leaves. We heard the sounds for several minutes before we saw anything. It was strange: we couldn't make out words, but it sounded like a sort of polite, easy-going conversation carried on in a garden just outside a window. Then three canoes came into view, with four or five men in each. It was Tom Barker all right. He was kneeling upright in the third canoe and turning his head from side to side, scouring the river for signs. There were two other Station officers with him, and several of Baba's villagers.

Out of the corner of my eye I saw Daddy crouched and staring past me at the old friends he'd turned into enemies.

"Are they looking for us?" Colin asked.

"Ssh!"

"Aren't we going to wave to them?"

"Keep it down, Colin, there's a good chap. We don't want old Barker spoiling our fun, do we?"

Slowly the canoes floated out of sight, but of course, we couldn't set off again because they were heading up river, where we wanted to go. So we waited half an hour before creeping out and paddling cautiously after them. We kept close to the mangroves, ready to dart for cover again. On we went, staring up the river until our eyes ached, and then we came to a point where the river seemed to divide. Instead of lots of little channels to left and right, there were two broad ones; or, maybe, one broad one flowing round a massive island of mangroves.

"Now which way?" Daddy murmured, sitting back with his paddle across his knees.

"You want cross river, Banner Pa," Alexander said. "To other side. Good to go this way."

And he pointed to the channel bearing to the right.

"I know what I want to do, lad. What I don't know is which way blasted Barker went."

"Yes, Pa, but blasted Barker, he think same."

"What?"

"He think you go up there."

"Yes. Yes, he probably does."

"So best to go the not good way," Alexander said, and he swung his arm round to point down the left channel.

"Hmm. Indeed, Alexander. My thought exactly."

So we cut across the river and headed left, and saw no more of Mr Barker and his rescue party. We did see more crocodiles, though, floating by or basking in groups on muddy banks. Most of the time they remained quite still, but occasionally they set off in a darting snap of tail and jaws.

"There you are," Daddy said, nodding at them. "What did I say?"

He had wedged the pram crossways at the back of the canoe, to provide a private space for what he called "the demands of nature". These were carried out with a great deal of nervousness and after an extremely careful survey of the river for the slightest signs of suspicious movement.

Just before nightfall, we tied up to a mangrove root and prepared to spend the hours of darkness afloat. We dug some biscuits and cake out of one of the rucksacks, and pretended it was a filling meal. Then we tried to sleep, making sure our arms and legs were tucked well inside the canoe. It wasn't easy. During the day, the surrounding trees occasionally crashed to the sound of monkeys swinging through and howling at each other, but at night the whole riverbank became alive with a peculiar whooping and moaning. Creatures we couldn't see and probably never would see.

halfway through the night, when I was at last managing to doze off, Alexander shook my arm gently.

"Ma," he whispered. "Ma, we got to untie canoe."

The tide had lifted us again. The rope had tightened and was dragging us down on one side. Daddy knew none of this. He was curled up in the bottom of the canoe, his feet resting on top of the pram, one arm wrapped around Colin, and the other around Hubert. He was snoring heavily, like one more strange creature of the night.

When we'd set things to rights, I tried to settle down again. Alexander took up a position at the front of the canoe, hugging his knees and gazing out over the dark water. I don't think he'd slept at all, and I had a feeling that he meant to watch over us till the sun came up.

"Alexander?" I said.

"Yes, Ma."

"Thank you."

"All right, Ma."

"And Alexander?"

"Yes, Ma."

"You don't have to call me Ma. You can call me by my name."

For a moment or two he was silent, and then he said my name, but softly, to himself, trying the word out and finding it strange.

CHAPTER EIGHT

Most of the next day we kept to the middle of the main river, though we couldn't be sure that's what it was. It might still dwindle away to nothing and leave us stranded again. During the afternoon we noticed the tops of mountains, purple and distant, above the line of trees.

"The mines at Okoja," said Daddy brightly. "We're making progress."

It was a long, slow day, but eventually the sun dropped towards the horizon, and a huge pale moon hung in the sky. We were looking for somewhere to stop for the night when we came across a clearing on the wooded bank. Little huts like those in Baba's village, but without the touches of brick or corrugated iron. People ran to the water's edge and shouted at us. We couldn't tell whether their shouting was friendly or not.

"What do you think, Alexander?" Daddy asked. "Good place to stop?"

"Not know, Banner Pa. Maybe not."

So we pressed on and the sun sank further. The brown river became streaked with pink and gold. I wondered if the maps told you how friendly the villages were. Did they mark them with little smiley faces? "If you ever find yourself floating aimlessly down the river with a pram in a canoe, you'll be all right here." Probably not. They probably didn't mark them at all because the villages weren't there long enough. People moved on, made new clearings and put up new huts.

"We'll see something soon," Daddy said. "We're bound to."

He made it sound as if some neat, bright hotel, with hot and cold water and fluffy towels, might be waiting for us round the next bend.

"Soon," he kept saying. "I have a feeling we'll see something soon."

I had a feeling, too – that the next bend would bring more mangroves and more trees, or maybe some tribe who had fast canoes and definitely wouldn't be marked on any map with smiley faces. The sky became a rich, deepening blue, and Alexander, sitting in the front of the canoe, was edged with the silver of the moon. We floated closer to the shore, and strained our eyes to make out some overhanging branch where we could tie up till daybreak.

"Well, well, well," Daddy said through the gloom. "What have we here?"

And there was our clearing.

"What did I say? I knew we'd find somewhere."

It was more than just a clearing. There were huts, too, and squares of yellow light at some of the doorways. One of them, right in the middle of the clearing, was much larger than the others, and painted white. It looked like a ghost house, a cottage lifted out of the English countryside and set down in Africa for a joke.

It wasn't only the hut that looked like a piece of England – the lady who lived in it, Mrs Henderson, did too. She was a missionary, bringing the word of God to the people of the Palm Coast, whether they wanted it or not. There was something formidable about her long black skirt and her hair, scraped back in a bun. She reminded me a bit of Aunt Sylvia.

No doubt it surprised her to see this strange party paddling up to her door with a pram in a canoe, but she didn't show it. She came down to the shore with a group of villagers and told them to haul the canoe on to dry land. Whenever she barked out an order, they jumped to it. She barked at us, too, a bit like a bad-tempered park attendant ticking off a family who'd spent an extra five minutes on the boating lake.

"What possessed you to be out on the river at this hour?" she said. "And with a child, too. Have you no sense?"

Daddy won't like that, I thought – a woman telling him off – but he was so relieved to be safe after all that time on the river that he managed to ignore it. When she ordered us into her hut, striding ahead and swinging her arms, he looked at me and winked.

"As daft as they say she is," he said.

"Do you know her, then?"

"I've heard of her. There were all sorts of stories about her back at the Station, but no one's seen her for years…"

"Come on," she shouted at us from the steps of her hut. "I'd rather you didn't waste more of my time gossiping."

She wheeled round and went into the hut. Daddy gave a little salute and we set off after her. The hut was raised on four thick poles, about five feet off the ground. It didn't have much in the way of decoration – a picture of the Queen, darkened and stained by damp, on the wall; a small embroidered piece of scripture above it (*What is man that thou art mindful of him?*). An old trunk stood in a corner with a couple of folding chairs propped against it. Plates, knives and forks had already been set on a small table.

"I always keep it set for a visitor," she

explained. "Although no one has called here for … well, for a very long time. My friends started cooking as soon as we saw you. They knew you'd want to eat. You *look* as if you want to eat," she added accusingly.

"Thank you," said Daddy, "we do."

"Then we shall eat now, and you can tell me what on earth you think you're up to."

She took a small brass bell from the table and shook it, making Colin jump. He stared at her with round eyes and clutched Hubert to his chest like a shield in case she should make a sudden dart at him. Mrs Henderson put two chairs up to the table, removed some books from the trunk and dragged that up too. Daddy leapt to her aid.

"I can manage," she said, almost elbowing him aside. "The little boy and the girl can have the chairs. You can sit yourself on the trunk."

A woman came smiling in with a blackened pot of something steaming.

"Thank you, Martha," said Mrs Henderson. "You are kindness itself, as usual."

Martha dumped the pot in the middle of the table, laughed to herself and lowered her head shyly. She made for the door and Alexander followed her.

"And where are you off to, young man?"

"Outside, Ma."

"Why?"

"I am house boy, Ma. Find something to

eat outside."

"House boy? We have no house boy non-sense here. You are my guest and you'll eat with us. Sit yourself on that trunk, next to the Big White Hunter there."

Daddy looked a little stung by that, but he sat down obediently, and watched her stack six or seven thick books to make a seat for herself at the end of the table.

"I shall sit on Charles Dickens," she said, lowering herself in a dignified manner. "I'm sure he won't mind."

Even Charles Dickens hadn't written enough to bring her up to our level. This didn't seem to bother her, though, and she closed her eyes and clasped her hands together.

"Grace," she announced.

Grace rang out, crisp and clear, and Colin looked on, his mouth gaping in amazement, as if he'd wandered into the quaint little abode of some folk tale witch.

"Now," said Mrs Henderson as she slapped the yellowish stew on our plates, "who are you?"

Daddy told her. He explained, more or less truthfully, how he'd left the Station in disgust at their treatment of him.

"You shouldn't be surprised," she said. "The British have a habit of treating people badly in this country. I have as little to do with them as I can."

"It's not because they're British," Daddy said. "It's because they're fools."

"We're all fools, man. You certainly are if you think you can drag three children through the mangrove swamps. Where are you going?"

"Somewhere as far from Barker and his cronies as possible," he declared. "To start afresh."

"Oh really? And how will you manage to live?"

"We'll grow things, I expect. Yes, we'll grow things."

"You've thought about how impossible it is to grow things here, have you?"

"Actually, things grow very quickly here."

"Not the things you *want* to grow. Clear a patch of ground and you'll have trees sprouting out of it in no time at all. *Trees*, not weeds."

If Mrs Henderson had been a man, he would've shouted at her, I'm sure, but the idea of an old woman spouting advice – well, that just amused him. He chortled, then changed the subject and asked her about herself. She told us her husband had brought her out to the Palm Coast after they were married, to help him bear witness to the people. This was before the War, and things were harder then.

"There was fever," she said in a matter-of-fact voice. "Yellow Jack. Half the time you were down with fever – and they couldn't cope with it the way they can now. The whites went down like flies. People like you," she said, pointing her fork at Daddy, "could only do eighteen months in West Africa before going on leave – if they survived that long. When Bernard died, I went home of course, but I found I was missing Africa. England's a dull place when you've lived a year or two out here…"

"Quite," said Daddy, nodding wisely. "Dull as ditch water."

"So I returned. There's important work to do, and I love the people."

After supper Mrs Henderson cleared out the small square room she used as a chapel. She hooked mosquito nets to the ceiling and tossed blankets on the floor. Daddy said it wouldn't be right to sleep in a chapel but she huffed and told him he was talking rubbish. When King David was on the run from Saul, she said, the priest gave him holy bread from the tabernacle. If the Lord didn't mind David eating the holy bread, He certainly wouldn't mind us sleeping on a chapel floor.

"Anyway," she said, "I shall throw you out when we have our services."

As I fell asleep, I kept thinking of her lonely life in this wilderness. The place at the table for visitors who never came… Yellow Jack fever… Poor Bernard dying all those years ago… How could she make a home in a country which had killed her husband? In the middle of nowhere. I didn't understand people like that. I'd never understand them.

Over the next few days Daddy kept walking to the river's edge, looking for signs of Tom Barker and seeing nothing. So we stayed. After all that travelling it was a relief to be in one place, to be at rest. We were more comfortable than we'd been for days. Our chapel bedroom was clean and dry, and because it was raised above the ground, there were fewer creepies to crawl over us. There were mosquitoes, of course, but we were used to them.

It wasn't all pleasantness and ease, though. Instead of being ordered about by one person, I now found myself ordered about by two. Mrs Henderson was as bossy as Daddy, if not worse. She got us all working, even Colin. He helped Daddy and Alexander to build fences and some new huts at the edge of the settlement. I thought I'd be doing the same but she had other plans for me.

"Come on, Natasha," she said one morning, appearing behind me on the veranda and clapping a hand on my shoulder. "You can make yourself useful."

She went down the steps and sat at the bottom with a large tin box beside her.

"What are we doing?" I asked.

"Waiting," she said, and she folded her arms.

I could see that she had no intention of telling me more, so I sat beside her and waited too.

"Tell me about yourself, Natasha," she said. "What do you want to do in life?"

"I don't know. To finish school in England, I suppose. If I ever see it again."

"And then what?"

"Well ... I'm not sure yet..."

My mind went blank for a moment, and before I could think of an answer, a man in crumpled shorts came shuffling up and sat at Mrs Henderson's feet. Without a word, he held out his hand to her. His thumb was so puffed up that he couldn't bend it.

"What's this, Michael?" she said. "Snake?"

Michael nodded so she opened the box, pulled out a square of cloth and a little bottle of something or other. She held his hand close to her eyes, like a fortune-teller reading his palm. Michael wriggled his toes and turned his head away, as if his swollen hand had nothing to do with him.

"There's a small knife in there somewhere, Natasha," she said. "Get it out for me, will you?"

I found the knife and handed it to her. Then I turned my head away, too. She finished with Michael, and he went away, smiling and nodding, and almost at once two women joined us at the bottom of the steps. One had twisted an ankle and the other was sweating and rolling her eyes with some sort of fever. We dealt with them and waited for others to come. And they did come, a constant queue of them. I began to think that this was a pretty unhealthy settlement – everyone seemed to have some illness or wound to attend to – until I realized they weren't all from the village. Most of them had emerged from the forest, from nearby settlements, I supposed, appearing like shadows and sitting patiently at the bottom of the steps till they were dealt with.

When I had taken a first-aid course at school I'd found that even the sight of pretend blood made me turn green. Miss Catchpole had forced my head between my knees to stop me fainting. Yet here I was, dabbing real blood from real wounds, not fainting, and feeling useful for the first time in my life.

CHAPTER NINE

I helped Mrs Henderson again over the next few days. Sometimes she told off her patients quite fiercely for their carelessness, but I came to see that it was firmness, not bossiness. Once or twice while we worked together, her wrinkled, leathery face broke into a tremendous smile. And I smiled back, surprised at finding myself so happy. One day, at about noon, when the sun was burning directly overhead, we were taking a short break and sharing some tea in the hut.

"Well, Natasha," said Mrs Henderson out of the blue, "what are we to do about your father?"

"What do you mean?"

"He's not a stupid man but he's a very proud and foolish one. Surely you must have noticed."

I sipped my tea and looked thoughtful.

"He's set off on this mad journey because he's been disappointed over some silly job," she went on. "Life is full of disappointments. You have to get used to them."

"He just wants to start something new," I said.

"So he drags his children into the wilderness. What about you?"

"Me?"

"You want to go back to England and study. Has he given that much thought?"

"Not exactly; he doesn't know…"

"Why not?"

"I … I haven't got round to mentioning it yet."

"What about Colin? Ronnie has no right to put him through this madness, has he?"

I shook my head but it made me feel as though I were betraying Daddy a little.

"I think we really ought to see if we can get you back to the Station, Natasha. I don't like the way they do things – running the country as if it's theirs – but I do believe that Colin will be safer with them, don't you?"

"Daddy'll never agree to it, Mrs Henderson."

"No, you're probably right. So perhaps the matter should be taken out of his hands."

I wasn't sure what she meant by that, but I had no chance to ask because just then we heard a jumble of raised voices outside. When we went to the door we saw half a dozen villagers gathered round Daddy, gesticulating and shouting.

"What is all this?" asked Mrs Henderson, and the shouting stopped at once.

"I have no idea," said Daddy, looking perplexed and put out. "We were working away on one of the huts and suddenly they started to sound off."

An elderly man stepped forward and spoke to Mrs Henderson in a sing-song voice. I couldn't understand what he said but it was obvious that he was complaining about something. Mrs Henderson frowned and listened.

"It seems you've found a better way of hut-building," she said to Daddy when he'd finished.

"Well, yes. I did make a few suggestions…"

"They've built their huts the same way for generations. How do you think they feel when some Big White Hunter comes along and starts changing things?"

"I wish you wouldn't call me that, Mrs Henderson. I'm merely trying to help. And I'm sure they'll see that it makes better sense if they do what I suggest…"

"Better sense? You're a fine one to talk about better sense."

"It's a matter of practicalities, madam."

"No. It's a matter of tradition. They build as they've always built and for their own good reasons. Please refrain from bossing these people around. You're not on the Station now."

I saw his eyes flash. I saw him clench his jaw. He opened his mouth to answer but she held up a hand to stop him.

"You can count yourself lucky that you offended them while I was around to sort things out…"

He didn't like that either. A *woman*, sorting things out for *him*?

"If you'd tried such a trick a little further into the forest, they wouldn't have sounded off, as you put it. They'd have taken matters into their own hands. Now, stop being foolish, man. You must apologize."

"Apologize?"

"House rules, Mr Banham. You are visitors here and you must stick to the rules. Not pompous white man's rules. My rules, African rules."

He gave her his slight smile and a little nod, but I knew he wouldn't let things rest at that. I could see what he was thinking as clearly as it was written in red ink on his forehead. *We're not staying here a moment longer than we have to. We shall go where there are no house rules; where a Banham can decide for himself what's best.*

Supper was so polite I could hardly bear it. Mrs Henderson sat on her pile of books, her back straight, no expression on her face, and Daddy sat opposite just the same, straight back and no expression. And he was deliberately well-behaved, to show how hurt he was. So we passed things up and down the table like people playing chess, in almost complete silence.

When it was over, Alexander and I helped clear away while Daddy sat with Colin on the top of the steps and told him a story. He became a different person, much more relaxed, when he told Colin stories. He made them up as he went along, and Colin always laughed and wriggled with delight. Sometimes he asked to hear one again, but Daddy could never remember them. He made them up and then forgot them. I could remember them, but they weren't meant for me.

When we'd finished clearing up, and I was standing at the door listening to Daddy, Mrs Henderson came up behind me and said that she had something to tell me. We went inside and sat together at her table.

"I'm afraid I've done something rather terrible," she said, looking directly into my eyes. "I feel awful about it but it had to be done. You're a sensible girl and I'm sure you'll understand. One day you'll understand if you don't now. Now, I think you might hate me for it."

"What is it, Mrs Henderson?"

"I've sent word to the Station. Sometime soon they'll probably turn up here, and they'll almost certainly take you back. I'm sorry, Natasha. It was jolly underhand of me but that boy needs to be properly cared for."

We could hear Colin giggling outside, having the time of his life.

"You're cross with me, I know," she said.

I wasn't cross – at least I don't think so – but I felt a sudden sadness and tiredness bear down on me.

"If only he'd decide to stay here – make himself useful – it wouldn't be so bad," she went on. "I could keep an eye on all of you. But he won't stay. He doesn't like house rules and he'll be off before long. I can see it in his eyes."

She took my hands and squeezed them, and I was so surprised that tears began to dribble down my face. I was thinking of her strange, crotchety kindness, and of Daddy, being forced back to confront Tom Barker, humiliated. I wanted us to go down two different paths at the same time – to stay and not to stay. I tried to say some of this but couldn't make the words come. She seemed to understand though, because she squeezed my hands harder and shook them, and asked me to forgive her. Then Alexander was there, holding a dish and wanting to know where it went. She stood up to tell him, all bright and businesslike, as if nothing had passed between us. When he'd bustled off, she lowered her voice.

"Whatever happens," she said, "perhaps one day you'll come back and see me."

"Yes, I'd like that," I said immediately. "It almost feels as if I belong here."

"Well, you've been very helpful, my dear. The work is certainly much easier with you around."

"Mrs Henderson, you don't think…"

"No, Natasha. You've got your whole life ahead of you. And I can't really take you away from Ronnie, can I?"

"He might not mind, though, if I stayed. He might think it was a good idea."

She smiled and shook her head gently.

"I think he'd mind a great deal," she said. "And I think you would, too. You can't really imagine saying goodbye to him, can you? And if we can get you back home to England, you'll be able to pick up your studies again, won't you?"

"I suppose so."

"Well, then. We'll leave it to the Lord to sort out, shall we?"

I thought I'd been asleep for hours, but it can't have been more than a few minutes. Angry voices were coming from the main room and someone was banging a fist on the table.

"What right have you to interfere?"

"I was thinking of the child…"

"My child, Mrs Henderson. *My* child. It

was none of your business."

He knew. He'd discovered what she'd done. But how? Surely she hadn't told him. I struggled out of my mosquito net and went quietly to the door. Opening it a fraction, I saw them almost nose to nose in the middle of the room, with Mrs Henderson staring up into Daddy's red face. Alexander was hovering around, like someone at a boxing match, ready to catch him in case she took a sudden swing at him. From the way her eyes flashed it looked as if she might.

"Do you think I'd sit here and watch you walk away," she was saying. "You have no idea of the dangers you might meet…"

"Madam, I have spent many years in Africa. Of course I know about the dangers. I also know…"

He stopped abruptly, catching sight of me at the door, and closed his eyes for a second. I shall never forget the look he gave me when he opened them again – so full of disappointment and contempt.

"You knew, Natasha," he said slowly. "You knew what she'd done."

"Don't take it out on her," said Mrs Henderson. "What was she to do?"

"She should have told me. She should have told her own father how you betrayed us. The decent, loyal thing."

"It wasn't like that, Daddy," I began, but he

cut me off.

"Don't interrupt. You didn't tell me, girl. You left that to the house boy."

"Alexander?"

Alexander had told him? I could hardly believe it. I turned to Alexander and saw his face twisted with anguish.

"Had to say, Ma," he said, lowering his head. "Banner Pa know what is best…"

"Don't explain yourself, boy!" Daddy shouted. "She's the one to do the explaining."

"I will not allow you to shout at her like that," said Mrs Henderson. "If you must shout, then shout at me. Natasha has done nothing…"

"Exactly! She has done nothing!"

He turned on his heel and pushed past me into the chapel. I never felt more wretched in my life. I thought he might leave, then and there, just as he'd left the Station. Out into the jungle in the pitch black of night. And if he did, what was I to do?

I faced Alexander again, choking with anger.

"Why did you tell him? You see what you've done?"

"But he boss, Ma. He look after us."

He was shifting from foot to foot and shaking his head. I wanted to scratch his face for what he'd done, but I felt Mrs Henderson take hold of my arm and pull me to her.

"Don't," she said. "He did what he thought was right. Just like I did and just like your father did."

I put my arms round her and cried into her bony shoulder.

"He's going to leave me behind…"

"Of course he's not."

"He doesn't want me."

"Oh, my dear, I don't know what to say. He's angry but he doesn't want to lose you. That's plain enough."

"No, he hates me."

She moved me to the table and made me sit. She knelt down beside me.

"You mustn't think that, Natasha," she said. "He needs you, and you must be brave and look after your little brother."

She sniffed and wiped her eyes with the back of her wrist.

"Oh dear, this is a funny do. I'm upset. I don't get upset. Bernard hardly ever saw me upset, you know. But what's to be done? If you go with him it's bad; if you stay it's worse. Oh, I could knock him on the head."

For some moments she rested her head on my lap. Then she sighed heavily and looked up at me.

"We must make the best of a bad job," she said. "I'll talk to him. I'll ask some of my friends to go with you, to guide you. And I'll pray for you all. That will be the best thing to do, Natasha. I'll pray for you and maybe God will plant a little sense in his thick head."

And with that she got up and went into the chapel, like St George going into the dragon's cave. He wouldn't have anything to do with her help.

"Don't be ridiculous, woman," he barked. "You would've turned me over to a bunch of fools. I don't call that help."

"If you won't think of yourself, then think of the children."

"The children are Banhams – they will survive."

"But surely…"

"I will ask one small favour of you, madam, and no more. You can, of course, refuse."

"What is it?"

"Since you seem so fond of sending messages, I would appreciate it if you sent one for me. To my sister in England. I shall leave you her address. Tell her that I have left the Station, that we are all well, that I will be in touch with her when we have found somewhere to live. I don't want her to worry."

With that he bowed stiffly and turned away. For the rest of the night he paced about, walking aimlessly from the chapel to the dining room, then out on to the veranda and back. I lay on my mattress, wide awake, listening as he clumped backwards and forwards, sighing and muttering to himself in the dark. Then, at first light, he told me to pack the things in the pram and get myself ready. It was the first thing he'd said to me for hours, and he said it rather stiffly and awkwardly.

So off we went again, Daddy pushing the pram like a man out for a walk in a park, Colin clinging to Alexander's back, still half asleep, and me dragging behind with one of the rucksacks. I took one last look at Mrs Henderson's odd little piece of England in the middle of the jungle, and saw her appear in the dark of her doorway. She moved to stand at the top of the steps with her hands clasped in front of her. At that distance she looked tired and frail. As we reached the far edge of the clearing, she waved slowly and called after us in a faint voice.

"I'll pray for you. I'll pray for all of you."

"Fat lot of good that'll do," Daddy muttered.

He plunged between a couple of bushes, barging the pram ahead of him. A fan of shiny paddle-shaped leaves flapped around him and swallowed him up.

CHAPTER TEN

I felt wretched, leaving Mrs Henderson like that, but no one seemed to notice how upset I was, so then I became angry.

"Where are we going?" I shouted at Daddy.

"We're simply leaving, Natasha," he said without even looking back. "And please don't raise your voice to me. It's not my fault."

"Well, it's certainly not mine. And it's not Colin's, and…"

He stopped suddenly and turned round. His mouth was set and his eyes were hard.

"I didn't want to be out here in the first place," I said as steadily as I could.

"No, Natasha. I will not have this. That woman was going to hand us over to Barker, and you knew about it, so please don't put the blame on to me."

"But you never ask what we want, do you?" I said, dumping down my rucksack. "It's your idea so we all have to go along with it, whether we like it or not."

"Oh, really? Then perhaps you'd be good enough to tell me what you do want."

"To be at home," I said after a deep breath. "I want to be at home."

"Your home is with me."

"This isn't home. This is nothing, nowhere. And we can't keep running away."

"We are not running away!" he roared.

Colin edged closer to Daddy and looked at me with a puzzled frown. Alexander stood stock still, embarrassed that I should dare to speak to the master like this.

"I thought you had more sense," Daddy went on, "that place was hers, not ours. If you think I'm going to hang around running errands for that old trout…"

"She's not an old trout!"

"That's enough! We're going on until we find our own place, and that's all there is to say about it. Now, pick up that rucksack and let's get moving."

I stared at him for a couple more seconds but it was useless to defy him any longer. I had no choice – I simply had to do as he said. So I swung the rucksack on my shoulder, and off we went again, in stony silence, Daddy forging angrily ahead and me dragging behind. After about twenty minutes they were so far on that I kept losing sight of them behind curtains of clinging leaves and green-black tree trunks.

"I'm not going to run to catch you up," I muttered. "So don't think it."

Then I stopped walking altogether and listened to them thrashing about ahead of me until I could hardly hear them.

It wasn't really planned – I just decided that I'd had enough of being ignored and ordered about. I thought I'd go back to Mrs Henderson. She'd take me in, I was sure she would, and Daddy could either come back for me, or go on by himself and leave me behind. It was up to him – I didn't care.

At least, I didn't care until my anger began to fade and the loneliness of the forest crept up on me. The trees towered above me, fleshy and threatening, and I couldn't make out the path properly. Nothing was straight. Everything was obstructed by twisting branches and criss-crossed with creepers, as if some invisible old witch knitted twigs and branches in front of me as I walked. I saw myself as a dot on a map, meandering all over the place.

I put the rucksack down and stopped to think – *Remember, Natasha, remember the way we came.* I tried to picture the little clearing where Mrs Henderson sat on her steps, patching up wounds and bathing sores. Then I changed direction and set off for where I thought she'd be, but it didn't make any difference. After a few struggling steps, the imaginary map altered in my head, and I was sure I was wrong again.

The forest was changing all around me. I sensed all sorts of living things nearby. Strange creatures, wild and uncertain. I imagined them closing on me, knowing I was alone. I heard rustling and scratching and the droning of bees. I could see the bees too, in a zigzagging cloud around the rotten trunk of a tree.

Part of the trunk moved in a streak of black and white. It moved and stopped, and I saw a creature clinging to the bark with thick hooked claws. It was striped like a badger, and was so tense and fierce that I couldn't help crying out at the sight of it. Immediately it scuttled sideways on the tree and turned to look straight at me. Wild. A dark head like a clump of rock. A wrinkled snout and a red mouth, gaping with daggered teeth. Points of black light fixed on me.

I took a half step back and it made a harsh coughing sound. Then I turned and ran. I pushed through leaves and creepers, terrified that it was snaking through the undergrowth after me, its needle teeth snapping at the backs of my legs. When I risked a look over my shoulder, I blundered into a bush. I rolled over, my hands covering my head and my knees drawn up to my chest.

Nothing happened. I stayed where I was for

a moment or two, gasping warm, damp air and feeling my heart knocking. There was a log nearby, soft with rot, and I sat down on it. I realized I'd left the rucksack behind, but had no intention of going back for it. Gradually the knocking in my chest eased.

I've escaped death at the jaws of some weird, tree-climbing badger, I thought. I'm still alive. Hopelessly lost and alone, but still alive.

There were clusters of dark, heavy fruit hanging from the bushes, and I wondered whether it would be safe to try some. Or would they leave me writhing on the ground in helpless agony? And then what? Would giant forest rats come? A leopard? An army of massive ants…?

One of the fruits blinked. It wasn't fruit at all but a face – a face watching me through fringes of leaves – and before I could move, half a dozen men eased out of the shadows and came towards me. My fingers dug into the soft log and I stood up slowly. But there was nothing to fear this time because I recognized one of them. It was Michael, the man whose hand I'd helped Mrs Henderson to patch. He was wearing the same crumpled shorts he'd worn then, and he was smiling at me.

"Lost," he said. "You lost."

I nodded. He nodded back and leaned comfortably against a short spear. Then he began to walk away, turning and signalling me to follow. The others fell in behind him. They were dressed in odds and ends of ill-fitting khaki shorts and old waistcoats and sleeveless shirts, as if they'd fallen on some large Englishman and shared out his clothes between them. They walked easily, and at a great pace, so I struggled to keep up. No one spoke.

They'll take me to Mrs Henderson, I thought. I'll be all right now.

We walked on and I kept looking about for signs that we getting nearer to the clearing.

"Be there soon?" I asked, but Michael didn't answer and we seemed to be more and more hemmed in by greenery.

Eventually he stopped and held up his hand. We waited, listening, and a voice came drifting through the leaves. I couldn't make out the words but I knew it well enough. It was Colin. They hadn't been taking me back to Mrs Henderson; they'd been looking for Daddy.

Michael moved some hanging fronds aside with his spear, and there they were, the three of them, sitting together against the pram.

"Look," cried Colin. "She's here! She's caught us up!"

As he walked over to them, some sort of change came over Michael. He seemed jumpy and nervous all of a sudden.

"You found her, my friend," Daddy said,

getting up and holding out his hand.

Michael ignored it and looked him straight in the eye. I walked over to the pram and Colin put his arms round me.

"We were just waiting for her to catch up," Daddy went on. "Is she all right?"

Michael answered in his own language. He spoke quickly and darted looks between Alexander and Daddy who smiled back at him.

"Slow down, old man. I can't keep up."

Alexander stood up too, and moved so that he was half behind Daddy and half in front of Colin and me.

"They from Enders Ma's village, sah," he said out of the corner of his mouth.

"I know that," Daddy said irritably. "What do they want? If she's sent them to help us…"

Michael spoke again, jabbing his spear in the air and making quick, urgent sounds in the back of his throat.

"Not come to help," Alexander explained. "They angry. Say you make Enders Ma angry too."

"Nonsense, Alexander. Tell them that is utter nonsense."

"Maybe not good tell them that, Pa."

"Well, what do they expect? They want me to say sorry, do they?"

"No. They want take Colin back. Also Natash. She good to them."

Michael and the others watched closely while all this was going on.

"We're not going back," said Daddy. "I don't care if it does make them angry. I am not trailing back to that woman and…"

"Not want you back, Banner Pa. Just them two child. You and me, sah, they want kill."

Daddy widened his eyes a little and put out his tongue to lick the sweat from his upper lip. I pulled Colin closer to me and squeezed him, partly to let him know I was still there, and partly to stop myself shaking.

"Tell them Henderson Ma would not want that," Daddy said at last.

Alexander said something to Michael who shook his head and answered with a growl.

"He say Enders Ma not know they kill us," Alexander said.

"I see. Then tell them we have gifts for them."

"But, Pa, I not think…"

"Tell them."

While Alexander explained this message, Daddy stepped back and took hold of the pram. Immediately Michael and the other men tensed and edged forward, watching as he rummaged about. One of them shouted something, but there was no need for Alexander to translate: what he meant was clear enough.

"Please, Banner Pa," whimpered Alexander. "You make them jump…"

"I'll make them jump all right," said Daddy.

"No," Michael shouted in English. "No gifts!"

And there was a revolver in Daddy's hand. His arm was pointing stiffly upwards. A shot rang out and wave after wave of sound echoed away through the jungle. Unseen birds screamed and flapped. Colin jerked in my arms. The men were crouching, arms over their heads. Daddy lowered the gun, aiming it straight at Michael.

"Can they count in English?" he asked steadily.

"Not know, Pa."

"Tell them I shall count to ten and then shoot them."

But they were already backing away. The bushes closed around them like curtains on a play, and we heard them crashing through the undergrowth and shouting at each other. I looked at Daddy. He was standing stiffly with the gun still stretched out in front of him and his eyes shut.

CHAPTER ELEVEN

Daddy said nothing about this encounter. He hardly mentioned me getting lost, either, pretending that I'd just lagged behind for a bit, and now we were all together again. Nothing to make a fuss about. Everything back to normal – if pushing a pram through untamed forest is normal.

But he did say, after a while, "Where's the rucksack?"

I told him I'd dropped it to escape a wild beast.

"Well, that's a pity because it had all our papers in it."

"Papers?"

"Passports and things. Still, no use crying over spilt milk."

Or nearly getting your leg bitten off by a savage animal, I thought. This time, though, I kept my thoughts to myself. The walking became more difficult. There were a few narrow tracks, just big enough to allow one foot in front of the other, and certainly not made for prams. Daddy and Alexander had to keep manhandling ours through tangled fingers of roots and clumps of fleshy, foul-smelling stalks.

"Not easy," Daddy said to Alexander with some satisfaction, "but it won't be easy for anyone following us either."

And they grinned at each other like a couple of boys sneaking off school.

Hours blurred into days, and light into darkness. We lost track of time. Occasionally there were villages where we were crowded and laughed at and welcomed. And when we weren't lucky enough to stumble on a village, we stopped in clearings and slept where we sat, with the glow of an oil lamp to hold back the night. Sometimes, between villages, the food ran out and we lived off the forest, eating the fruit which Alexander told us would be good. Most of the time he was right, but he made no allowance for English stomachs, and he would stand by bemused when we were struck down by the gripes and had to stagger off into the bushes.

Then there were two nights in the forest with no village between them. We were running out of other people, just as we'd run out of food. By this time we were grimy and slippery with sweat and our clothes clung awkwardly to our skin, though we were shaded from the worst of the sun by the canopy of leaves towering above us. We couldn't really see where we were heading – curtains of greenery obscured our way all the time – and I felt like Jonah in the belly of the fish, treading on and on in the dank gloom, hemmed in by ribs and veiny flesh, with no chance of getting out unless we were sicked up somewhere.

It was hard going for all of us, but poor Colin suffered the most. He was very tired and he hung on my back as limp as a rag, his face waxy pale, with two red spots on his cheeks. The toy monkey dangled from one hand and when it slipped out he would wriggle and moan until someone picked it up for him. Otherwise he made no sound. Once I asked Daddy if we might stop to rest, even though it was early morning – the best walking time of the day. He sighed and I knew he thought I was making a fuss over nothing.

"I think Colin needs to stop," I said.

"He's practically asleep. He'll be all right."

An hour later Hubert slipped out of Colin's hand and this time he didn't struggle to get him back.

"Colin?" I said, suddenly frightened.

Alexander ran past me calling, "Banner Pa, Banner Pa. We stop. Please stop."

Daddy left the pram and came hurrying back as I fell to my knees and Colin rolled off my shoulders on to the forest floor.

"Poor old boy," Daddy said, leaning over and cupping his hand to Colin's brow. "What's come over you?"

Colin's eyes were big and dark. He was still awake, but hardly knew where he was.

"Perhaps we ought to stop," Daddy said. "See what we can do for him."

That was little enough. We made him as comfortable as possible and I tried to keep him cool by fanning him with leaves. I watched the sweat pour off him, saw his little teeth chattering, and it made me feel so helpless. I'd been so pleased with myself when I'd helped Mrs Henderson with her surgeries – all those sick people, cured and sent on their way – but now that my little brother was sick I was powerless to do anything for him. He needed proper nursing, not someone who fished things out of a first-aid box and had no idea what they were for.

Eventually, Colin fell into a more peaceful kind of sleep, and I stayed by his side to watch over him. Daddy was leaning against the pram with his arms on his knees and his eyes closed. Alexander came and stood beside me, but I wouldn't look at him. We'd hardly exchanged a word since we left Mrs Henderson's village.

"I help," he said after a while.

"Don't bother."

"You angry with me."

I said nothing.

"Had to tell Banner Pa. Had to tell him. For the best…"

"Oh?" I said. "This is for the best, is it?"

"But I am house boy. Have to…"

"How can you be a house boy when there is no house? Are you stupid or something?"

I looked up at him, hoping that I'd hurt him. He stood still for a moment or two, then turned round and walked back to Daddy. Out of the corner of my eye I saw him bend and touch him on the knee.

"I go now," I heard him say. "I go, find someone."

"What?" said Daddy, struggling to his feet.

"I go, get help."

"You can't. Not on your own. We must stay together. You'll lose us…"

"No, sah. You stay here. I find you again. Now I go to village some place. Good people. Bring help."

He was already beginning to walk away, backwards, with imploring gestures for us to stay where we were. He looked at me before he turned and ran into the forest. I think he was hoping to see that I'd forgiven him. Perhaps I had – I can't remember – but I was too tired and sick with worry to think about forgiveness.

Just before nightfall, Daddy took the old oil lamp from the pram and – after cursing over several damp matches – managed to get it going.

"This'll keep most things at bay," he said.

It did keep most things at bay, but not the moths. They came batting against our faces, great, flapping things as big as playing cards, and they danced and sizzled in the air above the glass funnel. Outside our little circle of light, the blackness was thick and full of eerie sounds – sudden screams and low, rumbling growls. Daddy lifted Colin up and cradled him in his arms, whispering to him and stroking his brow. I watched them for a while, then wandered over to the pram and found Daddy's book, about the girl with my name. I took it to the lamp, let it fall open and started to read. I read about soldiers on a march somewhere in Russia. They'd stopped at a farm and were splashing about in a pond. Laughing, forgetting the war. I fell asleep reading.

Before it was fully light, we woke and found ourselves looking at each other across our little glade. The lamp was sputtering between us. Daddy fiddled with it and shook it but the oil had run out. I was stiff from leaning awkwardly against the remaining rucksack, and more tired than I'd been before I fell asleep. There were patches of green and gold light in the canopy of leaves above us. Daddy dropped the lamp, ran his hands through his hair and slumped to the ground. He seemed to fall asleep again almost at once. I closed my eyes, too.

The next thing I knew, someone else was speaking close by. A deeper voice this time, and strange. Alexander was standing by the cold lamp, looking down at us. Behind him stood a tall man in a camouflage jacket. His arms were folded and he had a rifle slung over his shoulder. I couldn't see his face because his head was framed in a patch of bright sky in the treetops, but something about him made me sit bolt upright, wide awake and frightened.

CHAPTER TWELVE

He seemed quite old – his short, tight curls were frosted with white – but he frightened me all the same. He stared as if he could make no sense of what he was seeing – an Englishman and a girl in a little clearing of trodden creepers; a cold lamp and an old pram. He began to argue with Daddy in broken English, turning occasionally to shout at Alexander and shake his rifle, an ancient weapon held together with tape. I couldn't follow everything he said, but it was clear enough that he was angry at being brought so far for so little.

Suddenly Colin let out a feeble cry. The man looked at him and blinked. He stopped shouting and knelt down to feel Colin's brow with a large, gentle hand.

"This what I tell you," Alexander said softly. "I tell you – sick boy."

Daddy mumbled something about fever, but

the man ignored him, lifted Colin in his arms and began to walk away through the undergrowth with him.

"Just one moment," Daddy called after him. "What do you think you're doing?"

But by then I knew that my brother was in no danger – at least, not from the man. I didn't know what the fever would do to him.

The man led us on for hour after hour, twisting and turning this way and that, and sometimes waiting, with Colin still in his arms, till we caught up with him. We didn't know where we were going, but it felt as if we were going *somewhere*, as if we had a proper destination at last.

Alexander was careful not to walk beside me – he either marched ahead or dropped respectfully behind – but I slowed after a while and waited for him to draw level.

"Thank you," I said. "Thank you for bringing help."

He looked steadily ahead and didn't respond.

"And I'm sorry for what I said, Alexander. I didn't really mean it. I was just upset."

"Colin get well," he said, beaming broadly. "He get well now."

We came out into the open, under the first leafless sky we'd seen for days, and found ourselves in a sandy clearing ringed by tall palms, with rows of huts, some squat, some big and sprawling. It was so bright it stung my eyes. This village was bigger and lighter than Mrs Henderson's, and didn't seem so remote or cut off. In fact, it was strung out along an uneven road which curved away into the trees. At the far end, just before it disappeared into the forest, was a low wooden building with a veranda, something like a store. Parked in its shadow was an old lorry with big round mud-guards covered in red dust. I stood still for a moment, looking at this new place and trying to take it all in. I could smell cooking smoke and there was salt on the breeze which touched my cheek. The sea. Yes, because over to the right I saw a neat line of fishing canoes resting on a ridge of waving grass, and beyond that a thin band of deep blue against the paler sky. It was strange to find ourselves so close to the sea. I thought we'd been moving steadily inland all the time, further and further away from the coast.

The man carried Colin straight down the track and turned towards one of the huts. Crowds of villagers had appeared and were streaming towards him from all directions, calling out to him, anxious to know what was going on. He gave a few short answers before shouldering his way into the hut. We lowered our heads and followed. In the gloom I could just make out a boy stretched out on the ground with his feet on a packing case. The man shouted at him and the boy waved his arms as he jumped to his feet. He dashed through the door to be met by a babble of questions outside.

The hut had grey mud walls and was full of warm air. A press of curious, silent faces at the door kept out most of the light. There was a cot in the corner and the man put Colin on that. He propped him up and gave him some water. Then he took a shirt from a box in the corner, soaked it and pressed it to Colin's head. He did all this in complete silence.

In a little while, the boy came back with an old woman in a long red cotton shift. She turned a stern, bony face to us, waved us out impatiently and knelt by the cot. Daddy didn't want to leave, but the man took him gently by the arm and guided him out. He smiled for the first time.

"Good now," he said soothingly. "She make good for him."

There was a considerable throng outside by now, mostly children who stared at us in open amazement. As soon as we stepped out of the hut, they started chattering again. One little girl stepped up to me and touched my sleeve. Then she put her dark fingers against my arm, and laughed back at her friends. I laughed, too. I couldn't help it. I believed the man. I believed that the stern-faced old woman would save Colin.

I asked her later how she'd done it, but she pressed her lips together and said nothing. Whatever it was, though, worked perfectly, and in a day or two he was up and about, playing with the other children. He became a great favourite with them, and so did Hubert who they sat in the pram to race along the sand and into the tiny waves. I watched them from the grassy ridge where they kept the canoes. It felt so peaceful – and strangely like some kind of homecoming.

Daddy, however, thought the place was too busy. Every day people were passing through, or stopping to trade, and he was sure that word of our arrival would eventually get back to the Station. So when I saw him looking at the old lorry by the store, I knew what he was thinking. Sure enough, he went to find Nduku – the man who had found us in the forest – and they spent half an hour together, leaning against the mudguards and chatting.

"It belongs to some German chappie," Daddy told me later. "No one seems to know where he is at the moment, but Nduku says he'll be back soon. Then we'll see."

"See what?" I asked, though I'd more or less guessed.

"See about moving on, of course."

A day or two later the German chappie turned up. He came walking down the road, a red-faced man in a tartan shirt, a dusty hat tied to his head by a cord, and a sack over his shoulder. We were sitting outside Nduku's hut while Daddy was applying some palm oil to the wheels of the pram. When the man caught sight of us he stopped in his tracks, squinted for a second or two and turned aside to spit. Daddy stood up and wiped his hands on his shorts.

"Greetings," he said, stretching out his hand. "The name's Banham, Ronnie Banham. And you're Fritz, I believe."

"Jacob. My name is Jacob," said the German chappie, darting glances from Daddy to the pram.

"Jacob. Of course. Nduku here tells me you're an engineer. You work for the mine at Okoja. Am I right?"

"Sometimes, yes," Jacob said with a dry laugh. "And what are you doing here?"

"Oh, just passing through. Heading north, probably."

"Probably, eh? And you've been looking at my lorry."

"Oh, is the lorry yours, then?"

"Of course it is. Nduku must've told you that. If you're heading north, you won't get very far in that."

Jacob nodded at the pram and laughed more heartily.

"So," he said, "you want me to drive you

north, do you? Well, you're lucky. I plan to take some of these fellows up to Okoja. Tomorrow, maybe next day. They want to be miners."

"Really?" said Daddy with a wink at me. "Well, that is lucky, isn't it?"

I didn't wink back.

Everybody gathered to wave us off. They gave us oil cakes, some fruit and an old petrol tin full of water. The children had made me a little bracelet of dried creeper with fish bones twisted in it. I gave them one of my pencils. Alexander sat in the back of the lorry, chatting to about a dozen young villagers who were being driven to the mines. Nestling between them and tied down with ropes was the pram. Daddy lifted Colin up and they jiggled about to make room for him. Then he clambered up himself, nodding and smiling and pretending to stagger which made them all laugh. I waited for him to help me up, but he was too busy making friends with the miners.

"You can sit in the cab with me if you like, Natasha," Jacob said, and he took his hat off and bowed.

The lorry coughed and shook, there was a great shout from the villagers, and off we went, bouncing and lurching down the road with Nduku running beside us and waving. His smiling face slipped past the window as we gathered speed and plunged into the forest.

"You don't look happy to be leaving," Jacob shouted above the drone of the engine.

"I liked it there," I said.

"Yes. It's very nice. But you have to move on."

"I don't know. I don't know why anyone would leave a village like that to work in the mines."

"Same as everyone else," Jacob laughed. "For money."

I could hear them shouting happily at each other behind us, and Daddy chortling along with them.

"Ronnie is a very determined man," Jacob said.

"That's what everyone says."

"But you don't want what he wants, I think."

"It doesn't really matter what I want, Jacob."

"No, no," he said. "It matters very much. So, tell me – what do you want?"

"Well," I said after a little thought, "after we left the Station we stayed with a missionary lady for a while…"

"Ah! Mrs Henderson."

"You know her?"

"Oh, yes." He gave his dry laugh again. "She's mad, of course. Mad but good. More people should be like her."

"Yes, they should. And that's what I want – to be like her…"

"Mad, you mean?"

"No. I mean helping people. You know, people who're sick."

"You want to be a doctor, Natasha? That's very good. And you are like Ronnie – determined – so one day you will be, I'm sure."

I considered this in silence for a while. Is that how he saw me? Like Daddy? I didn't particularly like the thought. I wanted to be me, not a copy of someone else.

"Anyway," I said eventually, "I can't be a doctor, can I? Or a nurse."

"Why not?"

"Because I can't go to school, and if I can't go to school I won't be able to train or anything."

He tipped his head forward and leaned against the steering wheel to look sideways at me. I thought he was making fun of me, but his jolly face had become serious. Then he straightened up and stared ahead at the road.

"When I was a boy," he said, "I wanted to travel. Far away. This was just after the War, you know, and I didn't want to stay in Germany. I wanted to see hot places."

"Like Africa?"

"Yes, and like South America, India … anywhere hot. But my mother didn't want this for me. She said I had to study. 'You be a sensible boy, Jacob,' she said. 'I don't want you running around all over the world.'"

I smiled to think of him as a boy, being ticked off by his mother.

"Then you're the exact opposite of me," I said. "You didn't want to study, and I don't want to travel."

"Not the *exact* opposite, Natasha, because we both wanted *something*."

"Did your mother change her mind?" I asked.

"No. So when I was old enough to look after myself, I simply ran away. Poor mother! She was very upset. She wrote to me: 'Dear Jacob, you have made your choice. I never want to see you again.'"

"Oh no, that's awful."

"Yes. Awful for both of us. But I went back for the first Christmas and she was happy to see me. She cried, I cried. Now I am in Germany every Christmas. She makes a fuss of me all the time. You see?"

"What?"

"It all works out in the end. You mustn't let a little thing like no school get in your way, Natasha."

I thought a lot about what Jacob said during that rocky journey. He made it all sound so simple and straightforward – *If you can't go to school, you have to find some other way* – and, for a while, I was cheered by this. But every time I heard the gales of laughter from the back of the truck, I realised there was a bigger problem facing me than having no school to go to. It was wearing baggy shorts and sitting next to a pram loaded with all our earthly belongings.

CHAPTER THIRTEEN

It took two days to reach Okoja and we only made three stops. The first was while we were still deep in the forest, so that Jacob could take a rest from driving. He sat upright, with his legs draped over the steering wheel, and didn't seem to sleep at all. Then, halfway through the next day, we called at a village to get more food and refill the cans with water. All this time the forest was thinning out, but so gradually that I hardly noticed. It was only when I had to shade my eyes from the sun flickering through the windscreen that I knew we were leaving the green gloom behind. The air became hotter and drier, and the forest was replaced by yellow grass and a huge flatness, broken only by the odd tree, like an abandoned umbrella on a deserted beach.

"Now you can see," Jacob said, pointing through the smeared glass. "Okoja is over there."

Through the wavery heat I saw a ridge of mountains in the distance – the same ones we'd seen from the river.

"How far?" I asked.

"More than it looks. Everything is further than you think out here. Couple of hundred miles, maybe."

The third stop was the last, but it wasn't in Okoja. The mountains were looming closer, and looking more and more solid, when Daddy slapped on the cabin roof. His face appeared, upside-down, at Jacob's window.

"Fritz, Fritz," he shouted. "Drop us here, will you, old man?"

"Here?" said Jacob, still driving. "Why stop here?"

"Because we don't want to go all the way to Okoja. Let us down, there's a good fellow."

Jacob ground the lorry to a halt. He heaved a sigh and swung out of the cab. Hooking his elbows over the side, he glared up at Daddy.

"You want to get out here?" he said slowly.

"If it's not too much bother."

"Ronnie, my friend, Okoja is a town. It has stores and food and drink and things to do. Here there is nothing, *nothing*."

"Yes, I know," said Daddy. "That's the trouble. Okoja is really too *big* for our purposes. Someone might find us there and we don't particularly want that. Also, my good friends here tell me we're close to the border. Can you confirm that, Fritz?"

"Yes," he said, nodding in the direction of a dark line of bushes on the horizon. "That's the border over there, and beyond it is Tumani. But listen to me, Ronnie. Tumani is independent. It's not run by Brits any more."

"Yes, I know this."

"So you can't just walk into it. They might not be so pleased to see you."

"Oh, I don't think they'll even notice," said Daddy. "You said yourself, there's really nothing here."

A few moments later, we were standing round the pram and watching the lorry forge through the long grass like a galleon. The young men in the back were standing and waving for all they were worth. Jacob's arm snaked out of the window in a slow and deliberate farewell.

"Now what are we going to do?" I said.

"Don't sound so grumpy, Natasha. Surely, you knew we couldn't go all the way to Okoja. Barker has contacts there."

"It's just that, as soon as we get to know anyone, they're whisked away," I said pathetically. "We'll probably never see Jacob again."

"I don't suppose that worries him much. Anyway, we'll meet some new people soon, won't we? We're going to strike out for a new life in a new country. Which is pretty exciting, isn't it, old chap?"

He ruffled Colin's hair, grasped the pram and pointed it in the direction of Tumani.

"Come on," he said brightly. "Let's get moving."

We walked towards the border for ages without appearing to get any closer. Then the dark bushes became more distinct, and we could see knolls of rock among them. After the constant juddering of the lorry, the silence of that huge, empty plain was incredible, so it came as something of a surprise when I heard a faint sound, like a horse blowing through its nose.

"Listen," I said, stopping. "I think there's someone over there."

We lifted our heads, straining to hear more. There was nothing to see but rocks and shrubs.

"Nothing," said Daddy. "Let's continue, shall we?"

Then the horse snorted again, and mingled with it was a tiny human voice. *Are you going to Scarborough Fair?* it sang. *Parsley, sage, rosemary and thyme…*

"Good grief," said Daddy. "It's English."

In fact, it was Irish, and it belonged to Dr Patrick. He came riding round a bush, singing to himself at the top of his voice until he spotted us, a group of heads staring at him over the long grass. He stopped short and sat there like a statue for almost a minute before urging his horse in our direction. I saw a pink, boyish face behind round glasses in wire frames. He reined in his horse and lifted his hat to wipe the top of his bald head. He squinted at the pram.

"Well, well, well," he said. "Well, well, well, well, well."

"Hello," said Daddy. "Can you tell us if we've crossed the border yet?"

"The border?"

"Yes. Are we in Tumani, or is this still the Palm Coast?"

"Let me see now," he said, climbing stiffly from his horse. "Perhaps. No, I can't be sure. It's hard to tell exactly where the border is."

"The name's Banham," Daddy said with a funny little bow. "This is Colin. Natasha. And Alexander, our house boy."

We nodded politely at each other.

"Pleased to meet you all, I'm sure. And my name is Patrick. Norman Patrick."

"Is there a village where we can get food and water, Norman? On the Tumani side? We want to get to Tumani."

"Well, there's my place," said Dr Patrick. "Not far – six miles or so, just round the Mountain. I'll show you, if you like."

"Most kind, most kind."

Dr Patrick asked Colin if he'd like a ride on the horse which, of course, he did. So he was hoisted up and off we went. As simple as that.

Heading for a new country. When we reached the bushes, Dr Patrick said he thought we were probably in Tumani.

"Yes," Daddy said, flinging out his arms. "We have arrived. This is the place – I feel in my bones. Our fresh start."

So we moved in with Dr Patrick, filling his little bungalow with more noise and fuss than he was used to. He was a retired medical man from County Cork and he had a lovely soft voice which sounded as if he was half-singing little questions all the time. Until we landed on him he lived alone, without even a house boy, in his untidy bungalow between the town of Bokanna and the Mountain. He called Bokanna a town but it was hardly bigger than Nduku's village. And the Mountain wasn't really a mountain, either – just a steep outcrop of red-brown boulders. It was about the size of a cathedral, and it had a stream of fresh water snaking round it. Dr Patrick called it the Mountain as a kind of joke, I think.

He told me once that he could have lived in Bokanna itself, but didn't much care for crowds. He went there sometimes to share a cup of tea with Joel, the half-Scottish, half-Lebanese owner of the trading post. They never said very much to each other, and Dr Patrick never stayed long.

He didn't utter one word of complaint

about us, but we must've been a terrible intrusion to him – Daddy so hearty and back-slapping all the time, and Colin trotting about and asking questions, and the visitors who came every day to look at us. Some gathered outside in small groups and just stared. Others banged on his door to see if we wanted to hire them to do jobs or to buy things.

To me Dr Patrick was always rather respectful and nervous, forever asking if there was anything I wanted and making sure that I was comfortable. ("Now are you sure you're quite comfortable, Natasha? Can I fetch you anything?") I don't think he was used to girls. Of course, what I actually wanted was to talk to him about medicine, but whenever I brought the subject up, Daddy seemed to wander by with his hands in the pockets of his massive shorts, and I just froze. I couldn't bear the thought of him mocking me, I suppose. Then I remembered what Jacob had said – *You mustn't let a little thing like no school get in your way, Natasha* – and I decided to find a way round the problem.

One morning, while we were having breakfast on the veranda, I told Daddy, in my sweetest, most concerned voice, that I was worried about school.

"I shouldn't think about it, old girl," he said. "They'll get along without you."

"I don't mean the school back in England,"

I said. "I mean I'm worried that there's no school at all, that I'm learning nothing."

"Nonsense. You're learning all sorts of things all the time."

"I don't want to go to school," muttered Colin. "Don't take any notice of her."

"But what happens when I grow up?" I went on. "I won't have an education."

"Of course you will," said Daddy. "It'll be unusual, certainly, but it will be an education."

"I don't want you to be ashamed of me because I'm ignorant, though."

He gave me a long, hard look, trying to work out whether I was joking or not.

"What do you need to know that you can't learn from books?" he asked.

"Well, you can't get everything from books. Like dancing. I used to have dancing lessons in England, you know."

"Good grief. Did you?" he said, sounding a little worried. "You've never mentioned it before."

I had mentioned it, of course, but he'd forgotten.

"I just don't want to let you down, Daddy," I said. "If only there was someone who could teach me some of the basics…"

He looked down at his plate and shook his head slowly. Then he sighed and left the table to wander round the bungalow deep in thought.

Later that afternoon, while I was busy sweeping dust off the veranda, Dr Patrick appeared at the door with a couple of books under his arm.

"Ronnie tells me you'd like some tuition," he said awkwardly.

"Tuition?" I said.

"Yes, he's asked me to teach you. I know, Natasha. It's a silly idea. I told him, I said, 'I'm a doctor, not a teacher,' but you know what Ronnie's like. He insisted."

He hadn't said a word to me – that wasn't the way Daddy did things – but he'd obviously thought about it, and chivvied Dr Pat into becoming a teacher. I put the broom down and we went indoors.

"I'm not sure what I *can* teach you, though," he said, dropping the books on the table. "I'm prepared to do my best, though. If it's what you want. Is it?"

"Oh, it is, Dr Pat. I'm just surprised that Daddy thought of it."

"Ah, well," he said, staring into the distance through the open door, "I believe he was worried that you might … well, that you might get involved in…"

He stopped.

"In what?" I said.

"In dancing."

I laughed out loud. I suppose he thought I might start pirouetting all over the place if I didn't have anything else to occupy my mind. And he couldn't cope with that – mincing about in frilly dresses is no way for a Banham to behave, even a second-class female Banham.

Dr Pat sat down uncomfortably and spread his hands.

"Well," he said, "I don't really know how to begin. I'm not very strong on maths, you know, and my English is a little eccentric…"

"Well," I said, looking him straight in the eye, "I'm sure there's something you can teach me."

"I'm really quite ignorant, Natasha. Unless it's horses or medicine."

I raised my eyebrows and smiled my sweetest smile at him.

"Medicine, Dr Pat?"

"Yes, but I can't teach you that, now, can I?"

"Why not?"

"I don't know. I'm not sure what Ronnie would have to say about that…"

"Well," I said. "We don't have to tell him exactly what we talk about, do we?"

Poor Dr Pat – he was always giving in to Banhams. Once he started talking about medicine though, his bumbling and nervousness disappeared. He stopped being so *polite* all the time, and that was a relief to both of us. He even began to tick me off when I made mistakes. ("Natasha, you daftie. Do you not think the problem could be with the ribs and not the chest?") After two or three lessons I could see myself back in London, wrapped against the cold in a student scarf and discussing fractures in a coffee bar.

Daddy took no interest in what we were doing. Once he stopped and looked over my shoulder at a picture of a skeleton in one of Dr Pat's fat books.

"Ah, science," he said. "Jolly good, jolly good."

And he ambled off, humming to himself.

One evening after dinner, he dropped into the seat next to Dr Patrick on the veranda and said it was time to move on.

"We've taken advantage of your hospitality for long enough," he said. "Time to be finding a place of our own."

I held my breath. A place of our own? Where? And what about my lessons? They can't stop now, I thought, they've only just started.

Dr Patrick nodded and sucked on his pipe.

"Well, Ronnie," he said, "you won't be going too far, I hope."

"No, no. Very close in fact. As soon as we set foot in Tumani I knew this was the place for us. There's a patch of good land where the stream winds round the Mountain. Thought it might be a good idea to build a house of our own there."

"Hmm, sounds good. Certainly, it does. But you'll take a proper look at the land first, Ronnie. If it's where I think it is it can get awful marshy and…"

"I've already looked at it, Pat," Daddy said, slapping him on his pink knee. "It's soft all right, but that makes the grass richer. Might do nicely for a few cows."

CHAPTER FOURTEEN

In little more than three weeks a kind of house appeared on the slope by the Mountain. Our house. Mountain Farm, Daddy called it. He was keen to get in as soon as possible, so we moved as soon as it had a roof. We slept on rush mats borrowed from Dr Pat, and wrapped ourselves in mosquito nets at night.

"We can rough it for a while," Daddy said. "It'll be worth it."

There was plenty of help. Dozens of people from neighbouring villages drifted by to lend a hand, and dozens more came to watch. They took to Daddy and would do anything he asked them. And he was in his element, striding about in his shorts and barking orders.

Before we started building, he spent hours kneeling on Dr Pat's veranda with a chart, and for the first few days he spread this out on the grass with a couple of rocks to weigh it down.

He kept wandering over to check on it, studying it with his head on one side, but the house didn't look anything like the one he'd drawn, and in the end he abandoned the chart. Instead he simply started in one corner and built outwards, not quite at right-angles, driving wooden stakes into the soft ground to hold one log on top of another, and plastering mud from the river bank in the gaps. All very rough and ready but it seemed to work.

Dr Patrick rode over once or twice to continue with the lessons and to see how we were getting on.

"I'm not sure," he said, shaking his bald head and wiping his glasses on his sleeve. "I'm not sure it's the driest or the *wisest* place to set up home."

"No, Pat," Daddy said, "it's an ideal spot; good grass and water nearby."

And he went back to work, chuckling to think that a mere doctor should try to teach him anything about building houses.

Sometimes we stopped work and stretched out on the grass to rest. At least, Daddy and I did. Alexander and Colin played football with some of the helpers. It was odd to see Alexander playing, like any other boy of his age. During our journey we had come to rely on him in so many ways – but he was still a boy, really. They made a ball out of knotted twine, and chased it, laughing and whooping. Part of me wanted to join in, but somehow I'd lost the habit of playing.

The more I learned about the human body, the more I realized how ignorant I was. Dr Pat included one or two English lessons and a bit of Geography (mostly about Ireland) just in case Daddy thought we did nothing but science. It wasn't really necessary, though. His attention was focused entirely on the house. When it was finished, it made a rather higgledy-piggledy picture, leaning in places where it shouldn't have leant. He meant it to have four walls – two long and two short – but he couldn't quite make them meet, so he had to squeeze in a fifth. The roof was thatched with thick stalks of yellow-grey grass cut from the nearby plains. This had been more successful than the rest because Daddy had allowed Alexander to take charge. Alexander used to thatch huts back in the Palm Coast so he knew how to keep the grass from sliding off or caving in, and how much of a gap to leave for smoke to wind its way out. All the same, Daddy couldn't resist adding a touch or two of his own.

"You haven't got enough grass on that, Alexander," he said, leaning on his fork. "That won't keep the rain out."

"Oh yes, Banner Pa. Think so."

"Nonsense. We need another load."

So they got another load and by the time they'd finished, the house looked like a sort of squat monster with a bad haircut. It wasn't quite as sturdy as it appeared. The wood at the base of the walls remained damp and soon began to rot, while the mud at the top cracked and fell away in lumps. Also, the whole thing seemed to be sinking slowly into the ground. It sagged like an old man, bent and depressed with life, or maybe just tired of his terrible haircut. The roof beams descended inch by inch, and Daddy kept banging his head on them. He didn't complain, of course, because that would have meant admitting he'd made a mistake.

We started to cultivate the ground even before the house was finished, planting yams and bananas and groundnuts. Things grew very easily. In fact, the problem was not to make our crops sprout, but to stop other things sprouting among them. A sort of umbrella tree sprang up everywhere, rather like Jack's beanstalk – as soon as your back was turned, there was another little umbrella plant ready to wind up to the sky. I spent hours weeding them out. They seemed to be especially fond of Mountain Farm, where the soil was so rich that even some of the logs in our walls began to grow leaves.

In a way all this was rather exciting, I suppose, but I still dreamed about England and found myself wishing for cold drizzle and buses and shops.

The capital of Tumani was, for some reason, also called Tumani, and Daddy decided to pay it a visit. He walked into Bokanna and caught a train which chugged for most of a day until it reached the heart of the country. There he presented himself to the British High Commissioner. "Bit of an old duffer," he told us afterwards, "but fairly helpful in his way." I couldn't help wondering what the High Commissioner told his family about Daddy. Maybe they got on well together – Daddy could be charming enough when he wanted to be.

The purpose of this trip was to get in touch with the Station back in Liberation, to sort out our papers and badger them to send some money owing to him.

"There's a telephone in Bokanna," he said, "but Barker is more likely to jump if he hears the High Commissioner on the blower."

While he was away, the rest of us were busy on the farm. I kept up the battle against the umbrella plants, and trudged backwards and forwards from the stream with water, and Colin and Alexander tried to keep the house from caving in on us. They propped branches against the walls and squeezed more mud between the logs. This was the job Colin enjoyed best of all. He also liked studying the endless lines of termites that marched around and sometimes through the house.

The termites took a great interest in us. In the middle of the house Daddy had made a pile of earth, about two feet high, which he topped with a couple of rough sections cut from a thick tree to form our dining table. Every evening we sat round it for dinner, and the termites stalked across, only wandering from their path to see what we were eating. This annoyed Daddy no end and he'd jump about, swishing them off in all directions and calling them all kinds of names. There was no stopping them, though. One breakaway group decided to build a little hill in one corner of the house. Nobody realized at first because they chose a spot quite close to Colin's bed and he leaned Hubert against it to hide it from prying eyes. It was taller than the table before Daddy noticed it. Then he stood over it with his hands on his hips.

"Of all the nerve," he said, and marched outside to get a shovel.

He came back to find Colin sitting on it and frowning like thunder.

"Out of the way, old son. I'm going to dig those beggars out."

"They're not beggars," Colin declared firmly. "They're my friends."

"Well, we can't leave them there, Colin."

"Why not? It's their home."

"It's our home, too, and if that thing gets much bigger we'll have to move out."

"I don't care, I don't care."

So the hill was saved, for a while, at least. It was almost three feet high before Colin agreed to *some* of it being removed. Daddy sliced the top off and carried it carefully outside so Colin's little friends could make their own fresh start. The flattened top he left behind became Colin's bedside table.

One day we walked to Joel's store in Bokanna to meet a small, stiff man with a sandy moustache who'd travelled all the way from the British High Commission in Tumani with Daddy's money. Daddy insisted on buying him a drink or two, so the two of them sat on a couple of sacks of flour while Daddy told him endless tales of Banhams past and present, and all about Mountain Farm.

"The best thing about the place, from my point of view," he said, "is that there's no one to tell me what to do."

"Really?" said the man, sucking the ends of his moustache. "Then you haven't met Abu yet, I take it?"

"Who?"

"Never mind. You'll meet him in the end, if you stay long enough."

"Oh, I'll stay all right. This place is in my

blood now."

While they talked, Alexander, Colin and I sat on Joel's porch and watched the world go by. Under the shade of an old thorn tree opposite we saw two men drinking palm wine from a large earthenware jug. They took it in turns, swig after swig, and when one of them tried to stand up, he staggered backwards into the tree and fell down again. Colin thought he'd done it on purpose, and laughed out loud.

"No," said Alexander. "Not funny, Colin. That make him do bad things."

Then there was laughter behind us, too. I looked over my shoulder at Daddy and his friend sitting on their sacks. Daddy must've said something really amusing, because the stiff little man rocked backwards and forwards until he clunked his head against a saucepan hanging from a beam. Colin gave Alexander a quizzical frown.

"What about that, Alex?" he asked. "Can we laugh at that?"

Colin and I were down at the stream, filling an old bath with water. At least, I was filling the bath – Colin was marching up and down in the water, swinging his arms and splashing for all he was worth.

"Don't you go too far," I told him. "You'll fall over and float out to sea."

"What would you do then, Nat?"

"I'd laugh."

"Alex said it's wrong to laugh when people fall over."

"It's wrong to laugh if they drink too much," I said. "Anyway, you have to be careful, because the stream runs into the river and the river runs down to the sea."

"Does it?"

"Yes, through the mangrove swamp. You don't want to end up there, do you?"

He didn't answer and I assumed he was thinking it over, but he was shielding his eyes and peering up the slope towards the house.

"Someone's come to see us, Nat," he said.

There were three of them. Two wore loose striped shirts down to their knees, and the third, who was leaning forward and craning his head round our door, was dressed in a neat bush shirt and long trousers. Even from that distance I could see that he was someone important. I grabbed the bath in one hand and Colin in the other and dragged them both out of the stream.

"Go and find Daddy and Alex," I said. "They're in the yam field."

"Why can't you go? I want to…"

"Go and find them, Colin. Tell them to come to the house."

I gave him a little push and off he trotted, grumbling that he was missing the fun. Then I wiped my hands on my shorts and made my way up the slope.

"Can I help?" I called. "Are you looking for someone?"

The man in the bush shirt backed out of the doorway and jumped round to face me. He looked shocked at my sudden appearance, but only for a moment.

"My name is Abu," he said, making a formal bow. "I am an officer of the Tumani Civil Service."

"How do you do?" I said.

"Very pleasantly, thank you," he said, and smiled.

He was quite short – the other two towered over him – and he wore glasses in thick brown frames which made him look studious. His companions arranged themselves behind him and watched me closely, one over each shoulder in steely silence. Abu didn't bother to introduce them. They looked rather alike and in time I came to think of them as twins – Abu's twin guardians.

"I have been visiting Bokanna," he explained, "to inspect the Trading Post. Joel told me you were living out here so I came to pay my respects."

"Won't you come in?" I said, gesturing at the door.

"Most kind, most kind," he said.

He folded his hands across his chest and went in, bowing and smiling. The twins stayed outside. I cleared my throat and tried to think of something to say, but before I could Daddy and Alexander came striding in with Colin in tow.

"What's all this?" Daddy said, flinging his hoe down and shooting me a glance.

Abu introduced himself again and held out his hand for Daddy to shake.

"Joel tells me you are from the Palm Coast," he said, taking a folded cloth from his pocket to wipe mud from his hand.

"We were, yes, but we've settled here."

"So I see, and you are most welcome, I'm sure, but I am wondering whether all the formalities have been completed."

"Formalities," said Daddy with a snort. "What formalities?"

"Well, this is Tumani. It is not a British colony…"

"You mean we have no right here? Is that it?"

"No, no. If you have paid for the land, there should be no problem…"

"Pay for it? But nobody wants it."

"I don't think that can be true. My government wants it. Indeed, my government already has it. But perhaps you are paying rent?"

"Of course we're not. You must know we're not."

"Then I can arrange it, if you like, Mr Banham. My government would be pleased to see you farm here, but the matter of rent must be settled first. Of course."

And the matter of rent was settled. Daddy huffed and bristled, but he could see that Abu was right: the land wasn't ours so it had to be paid for. He could pay. He had money. It was Palm Coast money but it was acceptable in Tumani. What were the terms? The terms were not bad and Daddy agreed as politely as he could. I knew he was seething inside, though, holding his breath and getting redder in the face. It wasn't the thought of the money that got under his skin. It was the fact that some stranger had turned up out of the blue to order him around.

"I will draw up some papers," Abu said, tapping the tips of his fingers together. "The next time I pass this way, I shall bring them for you to sign."

He smiled again, then bobbed his head and backed through the door. We heard him outside telling the twins off for leaning against our wall. Daddy hissed through his teeth and ran muddy fingers through his hair.

"Mealy-mouthed upstart," he breathed. "I don't like his manner. I don't like it at all."

He stalked outside to see them off. Lots of "nice to meet you's" from Abu and slight smiles from him. It took all his Service training to prevent him from planting his boot against Abu's backside and propelling him down the slope.

"Oh," said Abu just before he led the twins away, "one last thing. You have official papers, of course. Passports and a visa allowing you into our country."

"What?"

"I am sure you have but it is my job to ask."

"We have," said Daddy. "Indeed we have. Somewhere."

"Then I shall inspect them when next I call. Just to make sure everything is above board and shipshape. Goodbye, Mr Banham. Goodbye, miss."

We watched them walking sedately away until they were out of sight.

"A visa?" I asked. "We haven't got a visa, have we, Daddy? And we certainly haven't got passports."

"I'm well aware of that, Natasha," he snapped. "*Someone* left them in the jungle if you remember. I wasn't going to tell him that, though, was I?"

And he turned on his heel and stormed into the house.

This business of the papers bothered us all. I was afraid that we'd be thrown out and have to go trekking into the Palm Coast again. Daddy was simply worried that Abu would get the better of him. Later that night I saw him sitting at our dining table writing a letter, leaning over it with his arm crooked, as if he didn't want anyone to see what he was doing. When he'd finished he read it through and chortled softly. He was pleased with it, so I guessed he wouldn't be able to keep it to himself, and, sure enough, he called us together to hear it read out. It was to the High Commissioner in Tumani, reminding him of Daddy's recent visit and asking him – in a rather pushy way, I thought – to get a move on with the missing papers. It was also sprinkled with complaints about the way Abu had treated us. These were the things that made him chortle, and he read them out twice before tossing the letter to me.

"You can take this to Bokanna for me, Natasha," he said. "I'm sure Joel knows how to send letters off to the capital."

"By myself?" I said, surprised that he'd trust me with a mission like that.

"Well, I've got stacks to do here. I haven't got the time to swan off to Bokanna. Alex can go with you, though. I need a few things for the farm."

"I can manage by myself," I said shortly.

"You won't be able to bring things back without help," he said.

"Yes I will. I can take the pram."

"The pram? Nonsense," he snorted. "They won't fit in a pram."

"What won't?"

"Cattle."

"Cattle?"

"You can drive cattle, can't you, Alex?"

"Yes, sah," Alex said, his eyes twinkling.

"You want me to buy *cattle*?" I asked.

"Of course. I told you, didn't I?"

"No, you didn't tell me…"

"Well, I'm telling you now, if only you have the patience to listen. The farm is about ready for some cattle, I think. Three to start with, just to see how we get on. All right, Natasha? Don't sit there with your mouth open, child."

CHAPTER FIFTEEN

On the day we took Daddy's letter to Bokanna, Dr Pat turned up out of the blue and tagged along with us. As we walked I asked him what he thought about the papers.

"Is it serious, do you think?" I said.

"Ah, well, Natasha, who can say? Abu is a determined man."

He said no more but I took his silence as a bad sign. We'd have to get papers from somewhere or we'd be sent on our way. Or worse.

We sat on sacks of flour in Joel's store and looked out of the window at the splendours of the town. It didn't take us long – Bokanna only had two splendours. One was the store itself, and the other was the railway station, the last stop on a line that ran more than a hundred miles east from the capital. The station was nothing like the smoky vaults in London. It didn't even have a platform. The line just stopped by a couple of wooden sheds in a patch of dust darkened by oil. A huge green and black train had arrived that morning and was smoking and steaming in the heat while we watched.

The rest of Bokanna was a muddle of huts, some topped with thatch and some with sheets of corrugated iron. There was a sort of market – one or two people sitting in the shade of trees with their goods set out on rush mats and swishing at flies while they waited for customers.

It was strange to find a big store laden with such a variety of goods in a place like Bokanna. It was stacked not just with tins and boxes and bottles, rakes and shovels, but it had shelves neatly piled with weird hats, beautiful old saddles, coloured blankets – all sorts of things. I couldn't understand how they managed to sell any of this, but Dr Pat told me people came from miles around to shop there. They might travel two days, just to buy a roll of wire to stop their chickens from wandering.

"You can buy anything you need here," he said. "If Joel hasn't got it, he'll get it somehow. I don't know how he manages it, but he does."

"Anything at all, Dr Pat?"

"Oh, yes. After all, we've come to buy cows, haven't we?"

And so we had, though the way he said it made me think I might see the cows lined up on a shelf between the buckets and the Dixie cans.

Joel insisted on making us coffee and feeding us banana cakes. He was more than happy to see that Daddy's letter was properly sent.

"No work to do, Pat?" he asked as he bustled about. "You was only here a day or two back."

"Oh, you know," Dr Pat said, shifting about on his sack of flour. "I came for the company. And the exercise will do me no harm at all."

"Well, the cows is waiting out the back, if you want to take a look at 'em."

As soon as he heard this, Alexander jumped up and was halfway to the back door before Joel called him back.

"Hang on, hang on," he said.

He hesitated, and in the silence that followed I heard laughter and shouting outside.

"Is something the matter?" Dr Pat asked, glancing at the door.

"No, not really. But you better be careful, Pat. Something's … cropped up."

The something that had cropped up was Abu. He'd come to Bokanna on the same train we could see through the window.

"Ah, yes," said Dr Pat to himself. "I thought he might be here."

"Why?" I said, turning to him with a sudden uneasy feeling. "Why did you think he might be here?"

He looked at me, suddenly awkward, then bowed his head and spread his hands on his knees, and I knew then that he hadn't just turned up out of the blue that morning. Daddy had primed him.

"Daddy knew Abu might be here, didn't he?"

"Well, no, not exactly, Natasha. He wasn't *sure* about it…"

"Yes he was. He knew. That's why he wanted me to come, isn't it? So he can hide back at the farm."

"No, no, it wasn't like that. You see, Ronnie thought Abu would pester him about the papers. But Abu couldn't expect you…"

"Me. Exactly. A child. Nobody would expect a *child* to have papers. He used me, Dr Patrick, and you helped him."

I wanted to push him backwards off his sack of flour. Instead I turned away and walked out to the yard. Half a dozen men, arguing fiercely, stood round three cows tethered to a post. Abu was there, too, with the twins either side of him, arms folded, like bookends. When he saw me coming he grinned and bobbed his head, looking past me into the shadows of the store.

"He's not here," I said. "It's just me and Alex."

"No Mr Banham?" he said, pulling a sheet

of paper from his satchel. "What a pity. But perhaps you have brought the visa and your passports…"

"No."

"No?"

"I … I didn't know you'd be here. We've only come to collect some cows."

"So I understand, Miss Banham, but all these things have to be done properly. There is also the tax to pay…"

"Tax? What tax?"

"On the cows. Tax must be paid, you see, and it has not been paid."

"We didn't know about the tax either."

"Yes," he said with a little laugh. "There is so much you don't know about."

"Well, I know now so if you tell me how much it is I'll see that you get it."

"Yes. Certainly. I shall write it down for you."

"That is not right," one of the lookers-on called out. "If they cannot pay they cannot take the cows."

He pushed forward and made an angry grab at Abu's shoulder. Abu looked sharply at the hand on his shirt. Then at the man's face. The man let go and took a step back.

"We must not be so unfriendly," Abu told him coolly. "I am sure we can trust Mr Banham."

"But he sends a girl to buy his cattle," the

man persisted. "It is not right. We are not a British colony any more, but the President still bows to them."

"You are too impatient," Abu said after a moment's thought. "Things will change in time."

"What does that mean?"

"Perhaps there will be a new president some day. One who will not bow. You must wait and see, my friend."

"A new president?" said another voice, from behind me this time.

Dr Patrick had appeared in the doorway of the store.

"You mean there'll be a coup, don't you?" he said. "Isn't that it? There are plans to overthrow this government."

"If I knew anything about that, Dr Patrick," said Abu with a thin smile, "I certainly wouldn't tell you."

All at once the other men began talking again, very fast and with a lot more armwaving. Abu ignored them and took a pencil from his satchel. Pressing against his knee, he scribbled down some figures. Then he handed the paper to me with a flourish.

"There! This is what you owe."

"Thank you," I said. "But how do we pay? You haven't put an address."

"There is no need," he beamed. "I shall come to the farm again in two weeks' time. To check your papers. You can pay me then."

It took us ages to walk back to the farm. The cows wandered and stopped to chew at bushes and sometimes just stopped to think. Alexander skipped around them, talking to them in a low, sing-song voice and smacking them gently on their flanks. Dr Pat mooched along and occasionally he stopped to think, too, sighing and looking sorry for himself. He didn't actually chew at any bushes, but otherwise it was like having four cows to bring home.

"I'm sorry, Natasha," he mumbled eventually. "I shouldn't have come."

"No," I said. "You shouldn't."

"I just felt I had to keep an eye on you. To make sure you were all right."

"We *were* all right."

"Maybe if I'd explained, about my reasons for coming, I mean, you would've understood…"

"But you didn't explain, did you, Dr Pat?"

"Ah, well, I'm a poor weak man, Natasha. I can't stand up for myself."

"You let him boss you about."

"I do, I do. Don't we all?"

I looked at him shaking his head and dabbing the sweat from his brow, and smiled in spite of myself. He was right: we all let Daddy boss us about.

When we were halfway home and resting to let the cows chew in peace for a while, Alexander frowned and asked Dr Pat what a coup was.

"It's when someone takes over the government," said Dr Pat. "They don't like what's happening so they just take over. Sometimes by force."

"Why they not like?"

"Well, this president worked closely with the Brits. When Tumani became independent they had a big party and the Brits sent over some Duchess or other…"

"What is that?"

"Chief woman from England. Hat and white gloves. And she shook hands with everyone, and they took down one flag and ran up another one."

"So there was no fighting?" I said.

"No, no fighting. It was all very friendly and civilized. The trouble is, some people think it was *too* friendly. They think the President is too close to the Brits."

"And will there be fighting this time, Dr Pat?"

"It's just rumour, Natasha. It might not happen at all."

"But if it does, will there be fighting?"

"Well, I don't know. Probably not. It'll probably be all right."

"Yes," said Alexander, staring at the

ground between his feet. "I see fighting before. Bad. Bad for all people."

It had been bad for him, certainly. He'd lost everything because of fighting in the Palm Coast, until he ran into Daddy.

Daddy and Colin were putting in fence posts when we came ambling round the Mountain with the cows. They hurried towards us, waving their hats.

"Welcome, welcome," Daddy chortled and he flung his arms wide, delighted to see us back, and even more delighted to see the cows.

When he found out that Abu was coming in a fortnight for the papers, though, his mood changed immediately. And it worsened when he heard about the tax.

"He's making it up," he said. "There's no such thing."

"It was on a paper, Banner Pa," Alexander explained.

"That means nothing. I don't trust the man and I won't pay."

I told him he'd have to pay, because I'd promised, and he hit the roof. What right had I to make promises for him? Who did I think I was?

"Well, you should've gone yourself," I said. "You can't blame me because you were afraid to face Abu."

"What?"

He took half a step towards me and lifted his arm. He only lifted it a fraction, and immediately let it drop again, but I saw it, and the look on his face, and I knew that he meant to hit me. My heart was pounding but I stared back at him, feeling my nails dig into my palms. The muscles in his jaw were pulsing as he struggled to control himself.

"You disappoint me, Natasha," he said in a low voice. "You simply do not understand, do you?"

He crushed his hat back on his head and walked away, down the slope towards the stream, keeping his back straight and swinging his arms like a soldier. He walked as if he knew we were watching him.

"Ah now, Ronnie," said Dr Pat, trotting after him. "Don't be hard on the girl."

I heard Alexander let out a long breath beside me.

"Did you see that?" I asked in a whisper. "Did you see what he almost did?"

He didn't answer. His face was expressionless and he wouldn't meet my eye.

"I am house boy," he said, "Banner Pa's house boy."

"Really? I thought you were my *friend*, Alexander. I thought you'd be on my side."

"Bad thing to say him afraid. Make him feel bad."

"Good. I hope he does."

"Why you angry, Natash?" he said, looking at me at last. "You always cross."

"Didn't you see?" I asked, pointing fiercely at Daddy's disappearing back. "Didn't you see what he was going to do?"

"Wrong to say him afraid…"

"Oh forget it. If you're so worried about him, why don't you run after him and hold his hand? You just can't *see*, can you?"

Then I left him with the cows and stormed off for the house.

"What's the matter, Nat? Wait for me!" Colin called.

"Leave me alone, Colin. Just stay out here with Alexander, will you?"

I barged into the house and dropped to my knees, slamming my hands on the table and swallowing my breath to stop myself crying with rage. I sat in silence for an hour, thinking that I couldn't stand any more of this, that I'd just walk out and leave them to it.

"I'm wasting my life," I said out loud.

I remembered how I'd tried to run away before, back in the forests of the Palm Coast, and how I'd failed. This time it would be different, though. I would *plan* – do things properly. But the more I thought about it, the more tangled it all became. How far could I possibly get on my own, without papers or money? And what about Colin? Who would take care of him when I wasn't around? So I came to see

154

that I was stuck in Africa, that there was no way of leaving without hurting people. And then I did cry, silently and bitterly. I couldn't help it.

CHAPTER SIXTEEN

For some time I remained bad-tempered and on edge, partly because of the nasty after-taste of the row with Daddy, and partly because I was yearning to leave and knew that I couldn't. Daddy, of course, forgot about our quarrel almost immediately. He had more important things to worry about. As the day of Abu's visit drew closer, he became increasingly fretful that there was no sign of a reply from the High Commissioner in Tumani.

"Well, you know Africa, Ronnie," said Dr Pat. "These things can take ages."

"They can't, Pat. I made it clear enough in my letter. We need those papers urgently."

We were organized to make regular trips to Bokanna, to check on the post at Joel's store, and time after time each of us in turn came back empty-handed. Then, two days before the fateful visit, I was carrying water from the stream when a horse came trotting round the Mountain at an unusually brisk pace. I hurried up to the house, arriving as Dr Pat swung out of the saddle and burst inside with a bundle of letters and a package under his arm.

"Post! Post!" he yelled. "Ronnie, where are you?"

Most of the letters were rather grubby and looked as if they'd been languishing in the bottom of a sack for a couple of months, but the largest of them was clean and had an official crest on the envelope. Daddy snatched it up immediately. It was just what he'd been waiting for, two or three sheets of cream paper, typed in black and red. After reading intently for some moments, he gave a cry of triumph.

"Excellent, excellent! He's sent our papers – proper authorization from Liberation and a visa."

"And passports?" asked Dr Pat eagerly.

"No, but there's a covering note. 'Replacement passports to follow'. So Abu can stick that in his pipe and smoke it."

He put the papers on the table, weighed them down with a fork, and heaved a tremendous sigh.

"Jolly good," he said to himself. "Jolly good."

Then he took up the other letters. Most of them were from the Station and they came with a brief note from Tom Barker.

Dear Ronnie, it said, *I was so pleased to hear news of you all and to learn that you have found a home in Tumani. We feared you'd disappeared off the face of the Earth. If you ever get the chance to come this way again, you will look in and say hello, won't you? We miss you, and we won't try to keep you against your will, I promise! Regards to Colin and Natasha.*

Best wishes, Tom.

Daddy read it, chewing his lip, then tossed it down without a word. I managed to look at it later, and the sight of that familiar notepaper brought back all sorts of memories. Joseph pottering about our bungalow, and Mrs Sneeth gossiping while George fiddled with his pipe and said nothing. Mummy's grave.

There were also three small notes from Aunt Sylvia. Her letters were always short and to the point. Two were addressed to the whole family, so Daddy gave them to me to open, keeping the other back. The first was just newsy and chatty – plans for Christmas in London – but the second was full of anxious questions. Why had she heard nothing from us? Was anything wrong?

When I read this out, Daddy humphed and muttered, "Oh, nonsense! Why does she have to *fuss* so much?"

He must've worried about what she was thinking, though, because he took the third letter outside to read by himself. When he'd finished, he folded it up and put it in his shirt pocket. I guessed what was in it from the look on his face: his Big Sister had heard about us leaving the Station, and she wanted an explanation.

He took a pencil and some paper and sloped off to sit by the stream and write his reply. He was down there for ages, but when he came back he'd only written about half a side. He wouldn't tell us what he'd put.

It was only after supper that I remembered the package. When I looked at it, my heart gave a little leap. It was from Mrs Henderson. She'd sent it to the Station, and they'd forwarded it to us, unopened. I put it beside Daddy's plate but he wasn't interested.

"I've had enough news for one day, thank you, Natasha," he said. "And I certainly don't want to hear any more from that old bat."

"Then what shall I do with it?"

"Do what you like. I don't want to know."

So I opened it when the table had been cleared and the lamps lit, and it had such a beautiful, loving letter in it. She said she'd been thinking about us, and praying for us. One of her villagers had found my rucksack with all our papers and passports in it. She was sending them with her letter, in case we needed them again!

I read the letter several times before putting

it under my mattress for safe-keeping. I put the passports under there, too. And I didn't tell Daddy.

I lay awake for ages that night, watching the last twist of smoke from our fire curl up to the stars, and feeling that at last luck had turned my way. Because replacement passports were on their way from Tumani, weren't they? And weren't the originals safely under my mattress? I alone knew about them. I alone could use them... And perhaps Daddy would settle down now that he had his precious papers ... and, anyway, there was always Dr Pat to keep an eye on Colin...

And suddenly it no longer seemed so hopeless to dream of England.

Two days later Abu turned up to inspect our papers. Daddy greeted him with such great enthusiasm that he probably guessed everything was in order straightaway. When they were handed them over to him, I thought I caught a little twinge of disappointment in his face, a tiny twitch of the mouth. He stood by the front of the house, studying them through his heavy glasses.

"It says, 'Replacement passports to follow'," he said, looking up.

"Indeed," nodded Daddy. "Yes."

"Then you do not have passports?"

"Yes, we do. They're on their way. That's

what it says…"

"But I cannot *see* them, Mr Banham. You have a visa, certainly, and a nice letter from the High Commissioner, but no passports."

Daddy snorted and glared at the ground.

"Can't you understand plain English, man? The passports are on their way."

"Plain English doesn't count for much in Tumani, I'm afraid. I need to see passports, not a letter promising them."

They stared at each other intently for a moment or two.

I thought, Abu is going to win. He'll have us off Mountain Farm before the passports arrive. He'll see to it himself.

I thought, the passports are under my mattress.

I can't mention them. I can't.

"I have been very tolerant, Mr Banham," said Abu. "You have not always been fair with me but I have turned a blind eye." And then he shouted, so suddenly that it made Daddy blink and jump. "This must end now! Without passports you must leave!"

"But we can't. I mean … this is our home…"

"No. It is our home. You are guests. It is time for you to go elsewhere."

It was horribly quiet. A dense quietness. No one moving. Then there was a small, juddering sigh and Colin began to cry. Daddy looked at him hopelessly.

"No," I said. "Wait. We have got passports. Wait there and I'll fetch them."

"Saved at the eleventh hour, eh?" Daddy said last thing at night.

His voice came to me through the rush screen which divided our sleeping spaces. It was the first civil thing he'd said to me for days, and he'd waited till the lamps were out and the house was silent before he said it. I didn't respond.

"Anyway, well done, old girl," he said.

I heard him turn over on his mattress and sigh. He didn't ask why I hadn't mentioned the passports before Abu turned up. For a brief while I wondered whether he'd guessed what I'd had in mind – that I'd had my own plans for those passports. But I didn't spend long wondering. I knew he'd never ask me, and, anyway, I felt too wretched to care what he thought.

I remembered again Jacob saying to me, "You mustn't let a little thing like no school get in your way, Natasha." And what had I done? I'd thrown away the chance to make a life of my own. I'd let Daddy's dream wipe out my own. Again.

Only when the sound of his contented snoring told me he was asleep, did I allow myself to cry. And I cried until I slept, too.

* * *

When the new passports came two days later, I could hardly bear to look at them. It just seemed so cruel for them to turn up like that, when it didn't matter any more. Of course, I couldn't say why I was so upset. I thought about telling Dr Pat, because for a while I felt the need to talk to someone, but in the end I didn't. I was still a little unsure of him after that trip to Joel's store, I suppose. Besides, there was no point moaning. Luck had turned her back on me, and when that happens, Aunt Sylvia always said, you just get on with life. So that's what I tried to do.

The umbrella plants kept coming up, and we kept weeding them out, and trudging up and down to the stream for water. Dr Pat came several times a week, sometimes just to talk and sometimes to continue with my lessons. Things settled down.

Then Daddy bought some more cows and a bull. Abu, of course, charged tax on them, and Daddy flew into a rage.

"It's absolutely ridiculous!" he shouted. "He's making this tax business up."

He stamped in and out of the house, purple in the face and clenching his fists. It frightened Colin so much that he crept up to me and held my hand.

"The man's a crook, nothing but a crook! Well, we shall see, we shall see. He can come round for his money and see what he gets instead!"

He kicked over a bucket of stream water standing by the door and it sloshed over the end of his mattress. Then he swore, heaved the mattress outside and flung it as far as he could. It was bouncing down the slope and he was running after it and lunging at it with his boot when Dr Pat turned up.

"What on earth's got into him?" he asked mildly.

"Abu," I said.

Dr Pat had to hold Daddy by his shoulders and shout in his face before he'd calm down.

"For goodness' sake, Ronnie, will you listen to yourself? Now take a deep breath, man, and relax!"

I'd never heard Pat raise his voice like that before, and it rather startled me. I think it startled him, too, because his hands shook for a long time afterwards. Daddy intended to boot Abu all the way down the slope and into the stream, like the mattress, but Pat persuaded him to pour his anger into another letter of complaint to the High Commissioner instead.

"This Abu business is getting under his skin," Dr Pat said to me when things had settled down. "We'll have to keep an eye on him, Natasha."

When Abu came for the tax, a day or two later, Daddy remained cool and distant. He didn't kick him and paid up without a fuss, even giving him a wave as he left.

"Just you wait, you beggar," he said through his teeth, watching Abu and the twins trudge off round the Mountain. "Just you wait till my letter gets to Tumani."

After lunch, Colin was jabbering on about anything and everything, as usual, and I was half listening, when he suddenly started talking about the man who fell over. At first I didn't know what he meant.

"Yes, you do, Nat," he said. "When those men were drinking in Bokanna, and one of them fell over."

"What about it?"

"Daddy's got a jug like they had. I saw it."

"Well, we've got two or three jugs around here…"

"No. It was the same as those men had. And he keeps it hidden, so we don't know about it."

I changed the subject and sent him out to the yam patch, so I could think about what he'd said. The jug we'd seen in Bokanna was used for palm wine. Some of the men there drank the stuff until it made them silly and incapable. And sometimes wild with rage. Is that what Daddy was doing? Drinking? It might explain his sudden rage at the thought of Abu. There was no harm in him having a jug like that, of course, but why didn't he want us to know about it?

The next time Dr Pat came over for a lesson, I mentioned it to him. We were sitting under one of the trees at the side of the house, looking at a picture of a skeleton. A sheet was hanging from the lower branches to shade us from the sun. Dr Pat pointed to one bone after another and asked me to name them. I did about five, then my mind went blank and I just sat there, staring at the grass.

"Come on," said Dr Pat. "You know this perfectly well, Natasha. What's the matter with you?"

I told him about the drinking, hoping that he'd simply smile and tell me there was nothing to worry about. He didn't, though. He frowned and rubbed the top of his head with the flat of his hand.

"Well," he said, "it may be nothing, of course. A little drink after a hard day's work."

"Then why does he hide the jug?" I said.

He looked at me for a moment or two, as if he were trying to read something in my face.

"You've grown up a lot in the last few months, Natasha," he said. "I won't pretend it's not a bit worrying. Chances are there's no harm in it, but it might be a good idea to keep your eyes open, just in case."

"Keep my eyes open for what?"

"Oh, anything strange. Odd behaviour. That sort of thing."

"But he's always doing odd things. He

always has done."

"Well, anything a bit different."

"Like kicking his mattress out of the house?"

At that moment Daddy came strolling round the side of the house, deep in thought, his hands in his pockets.

"Ah, Ronnie," said Dr Pat quickly. "You've come to join our school, have you?"

Daddy ignored him. He plomped himself down, stretched out in our shade and stared up at the tree.

"I've just been down to the stream," he announced. "Have you noticed how it runs in a wide bend round the mountain?"

"Well, of course. It always has done."

"You know, Pat, if we blocked it off and built a channel for it, we could make it run down the slope much closer to the house."

"Could we?"

"Of course," said Daddy, hauling himself up and leaning on one elbow. "And there'd be no need to dig a channel all the way. Once we got it flowing in a new direction, it would rejoin the bed of the old stream further down. What do you think?"

Dr Pat hummed and mumbled and advised him to be careful.

"Be careful of what, Pat? A few days' hard labour and we could have running water at our own door. What could be simpler than that?"

"Well, for one thing the authorities might not like it, Ronnie. They've probably got that stream on a map somewhere."

"By the authorities you mean Abu, I suppose. Believe me, I have no intention of letting that little tick stop me."

"But if you change their map without asking…"

"Nonsense. A piddling stream like that? Who's going to know?"

Dr Pat opened his mouth to speak, but by this time Daddy was in full flow.

"It makes complete sense. We waste hours trudging backwards and forwards for water. A little bit of light engineering work and we can get the stream to come to our door."

"A little bit of light engineering work, Ronnie, and you could get Abu to come to your door, too…"

"Oh, stop wittering. It'll be all right, I tell you."

Digging started two days later, about a quarter of a mile from the house where the stream ran closest to the Mountain. As usual, there was no need to ask for help. News of the scheme had filtered into the neighbouring villages and a crowd of curious boys turned up to see what was going on. Daddy marked out the new channel for them with a pointed stick.

"We dig along here," he told them, waving

his stick like a general. "About thirty yards or so should do it. We don't dig here, though."

He tapped the ground by the bank of the stream.

"We don't dig here because we don't want the water to flow until we're ready for it. So we leave a sort of wall, do you see? Then, when I give the word, we knock this wall down and Bob's your uncle – we shall have a new stream."

"You see?" Alexander said to the crowd of volunteers. "Uncle Bob, Uncle Bob."

"The new stream will run along our channel, over towards the house," Daddy went on, "and then it will trickle away and find its own direction. Any questions?"

There were no questions so they set to work. Daddy was in his element, shouting out orders and marching up and down while they dug.

"No, no. Pile up the earth on this side. That will prevent the water running down the slope too soon. That's it. Keep at it."

They worked so hard that, by the end of the first day, the channel was almost complete. It would've been possible to finish the job then and there, but the light was fading fast and Daddy wanted a good view of the stream changing direction, so he called a halt.

"Back here tomorrow morning," he said cheerfully, "and we shall finish the last bit and see what happens."

The boys went off, pleased with their day's work, and we stood for a while looking at the new channel and the piles of earth on the downward slope. Daddy jumped in and trod up and down – yes, yes, quite satisfactory. He prodded the strip of land between the channel and the stream – should hold until tomorrow; yes, yes, not a bad job; not bad at all. Then he hoisted Colin on to his shoulders and we trailed back to the house for dinner. They strode ahead, full of talk about how exciting it was all going to be and what a clever plan it was. I followed a pace or two behind, not sure whether it really was a brilliant idea, or the "something odd" Dr Pat had told me to look out for.

CHAPTER SEVENTEEN

Next morning Daddy stood in the trench, leaning on an axe, and we formed a little group looking down at him.

"If something stands in your way," he declared, "you don't give up; you turn it to your advantage. And that is exactly what we've done here on Mountain Farm."

Then he swung the axe while the helpers cheered and Colin threw his hat in the air. Some crumbs of earth trickled into the trench at his feet and that was all. He gave it another whack but it still wasn't enough, and two or three boys had to jump in beside him and set to with shovels. At last a heavy clod tumbled down, followed by the first spill of water from the stream.

"Hurrah," shouted Colin. "Hurrah for Daddy!"

The water began to gush and they all

scrambled out of the trench, laughing and shouting. Soon it was pouring in and rushing along the bottom in the direction of the house.

"Now watch," said Daddy. "It'll flow out of the other end and find its own way. There it goes! Clean water to our very door. See, see!"

We saw. It flattened out, forming first a puddle, then a small pond and then rolling on, straight for the house.

"Blast!" murmured Daddy, walking jerkily after it.

As the first wave broke against the side of the house we started to run. It was pointless, really – all we could do was watch it happen, watch the new stream gather against the wall, slop through the back door and disappear into our home. The boys thought this was great fun. They hooted and turned cartwheels.

"Stop it!" shouted Daddy. "Stop mucking around, will you!"

"It is all right, Banner Pa," Alexander called, sprinting to the front of the house. "It is coming out again!"

The stream ran straight through the house, in at the back and out at the front, carrying some pots and pans and one of Colin's shirts with it. Daddy looked on aghast. I held my breath – I could see another explosion of rage coming – but he simply stood there for a while, like a statue, while everyone else skipped round to the front of the house to see the stream flowing out. Then he planted his hands on his hips and breathed hard through his nose.

"All right," he said in a strangely calm voice. "If that's the way it wants to go then let it. Let it!"

"But how can we live in a house with water running through it?" I asked.

"You'll see. I won't be defeated by this, you know, Natasha. We wanted to get the water to the house and that's what we've got – running water, as close as you could want it."

When the helpers had gone, Colin and I carried out all our wet things and spread them in the sun to dry. Daddy and Alexander spent the rest of the day gouging a sort of gutter through the house so that the stream didn't spread itself too wide. They put boards across it, packed with earth, to make a couple of indoor bridges. The water, of course, continued to run while they did this, so they had mud up to their armpits by the time they'd finished.

"Now we can help ourselves to water whenever we want," Daddy said.

"But we have to paddle to get in and out," I pointed out.

"We'll sort that out tomorrow, won't we Alex? Actually, this is far better than the original plan."

He didn't look as delighted as he sounded,

though. His face was streaked with mud and I thought he seemed tired and rather lost. He wandered outside – for some air, he said – and I thought about his hidden jar of palm wine.

That night I lay awake, my limbs tingling with tiredness, and listened to the familiar night sounds – Daddy snoring, Alexander humming himself quietly to sleep, the occasional scratch of insects. And now, beneath it all, the gurgling of dark water, like some gloomy song that had no end. When I fell asleep I dreamed again of England in the rain.

The stream proved a big attraction and people came miles to see it. The boldest of them ventured right up to the door and peered in. I was convinced that Dr Pat would see it as evidence of Daddy's drinking, but even he was impressed.

"Very clever, Ronnie," he chuckled. "Very clever."

"Of course it's clever, Pat," Daddy said. "It was built by a Banham."

So now, instead of regular walks down to the stream, we could fill our pots and pans from the water which ran beneath our feet. It took a while to get used to though, and each of us in turn forgot the stream was there and stumbled into it, usually first thing in the morning. But we did get used to it and, once again, things settled down.

One evening I breezed into the house and saw Daddy kneeling by the wall with his back to me. He'd pulled away a lump of the wall, a block of dried mud about the size of three bricks, and he was holding the earthenware jug in his hands. It shocked me to see him there, stooped and furtive, and for a while I could hardly move. I almost called out to him, just to see what he'd say, but decided against it and slipped away as silently as I could.

Later he took one of the lamps and said he was going up to look at the banana patch. While he was gone I pulled the block of mud out of the wall, but I found nothing. The jug had gone.

Every couple of weeks, Alexander and I loaded some baskets with produce and slung them over the back of one of the cows to take them to Joel's store. He'd been buying our stuff for quite some time and I always volunteered to make the trip to Bokanna because I enjoyed the leisurely walk, and the chance to talk to Alexander along the way without Daddy butting in. Whenever I asked Alexander a question on the farm, Daddy used to answer for him. ("Of course you don't miss the Palm Coast, do you, Alex? You're too busy here.") Alexander didn't seem to mind this: as far as he was concerned, being Banham Pa's house boy meant that Banham Pa did your thinking for you. On these walks into town though, he was different – more relaxed and talkative. He would tell me about his life in the Palm Coast, and ask me about England. He loved the idea of England, in spite of Daddy telling him what a dreadful place it was all the time.

When we got to Bokanna, we did what we usually did – tethered the cow and unslung the baskets, carrying them into the store and calling out for Joel. It was dark inside after the glare of the journey and we couldn't see him.

"Joel!" I shouted. "Fresh delivery from Mountain Farm! Are you there?"

We spread the produce on the floor so he could look at it. Then I made for the flour sacks where we usually sat to watch him cast an eye over our stuff and work out a price. This time, though, someone was already in our place. It was Abu, smiling patiently and swishing at flies with a short stick. The twins stood behind him with their arms folded.

"Miss Banham," he said. "How fortunate. I was coming to see you during my visit, but perhaps you can take a message to your esteemed father and save me the trouble."

"Oh," I said. "Then you know, do you?"

"About the stream? Of course. *Everyone* knows about the stream."

"It is all right," Alexander said quietly over my shoulder. "Good stream. Nothing wrong."

This startled me a little. Alexander generally

tried to merge into the background when there were other people about, especially if they were as grand as Abu. He hardly ever offered an opinion.

"Nothing wrong?" said Abu, clicking off his smile and staring straight at him. "You think there is nothing wrong in changing the map without consulting me?"

Alexander didn't answer.

"I didn't know the stream was on any map," I said.

"It will be. It soon will be," he snapped, then smiled again. "Things are changing here. People won't always put up with foreigners who take the law into their own hands."

"We didn't," I said. "I mean, we only moved a tiny stream. Hardly worth worrying about."

Abu stood up and walked slowly towards the stuff we'd spread on the floor. He stretched out his foot and rocked a clutch of bananas with the end of his toe.

"All these things," he said. "They really do not belong to you, you know. You come here and set up as farmers…"

"But we pay rent."

"Yes. You pay rent. But soon rent will not be enough."

He clicked his fingers at the twins who came to life and strode towards the door. They stood aside to let Abu through, but he paused and turned back before doing so.

"Tell Banham I shall visit in three days' time," he said. "I must see this stream for myself."

When he'd gone, Joel emerged from the shadows somewhere and stood beside me, wringing his hands.

"You better tell Ronnie to be careful," he said.

"You know Daddy," I told him. "It's not his way to be careful."

"Maybe not, but I can't buy your things if Abu don't like it."

CHAPTER EIGHTEEN

We found Daddy in good humour when we got back from Bokanna. So Colin and Alexander were happy too, because, as usual, their mood reflected his. Even the threat of Abu's visit didn't seem to dampen his spirits.

"Let him come," he said, placing one foot on a stool and striking a military attitude. "He doesn't worry me. Not one tiny bit."

"He doesn't worry us," echoed Colin. "Not one tiny bit."

"You're right, old man. And to prove it, we're going to have a party. Tomorrow night. We shall drink to our new water supply and the continuing success of Mountain Farm."

I didn't believe all this bluster. I was convinced that Abu's message had worried him. It certainly worried me.

If I'd known then what Abu's visit was really about, I would have worried a great deal more.

In the morning Daddy sent me over to Dr Pat with an invitation to join the celebrations. I was pleased enough to go. It was a relief to get off the farm and away from all his high spirits. I found Dr Pat asleep on his veranda with a book over his face.

"Ah, well," he said when I explained about the party, "the stream was a clever plan. Ronnie must be pleased with himself."

"Pleased? He's beside himself. And he keeps singing. I won't be able to stand it if you don't come."

He smiled and picked up his hat, but something told me he wasn't very keen on the idea. I thought it was because I'd just woken him up, but it turned out to be rather more than that. He climbed on his horse and swung me up behind him. We rode on in silence for a while, and I watched the back of his neck, wondering what sort of expression he had on his face. Thoughtful, I guessed.

"You're very quiet, Pat," I said.

"Well, yes, I suppose I am."

"What's the matter?"

He didn't answer immediately. Then he said, "You say Abu's coming to see the stream. How was he when you left him?"

"A bit grim. I think he's still angry about those passports. Joel says he might try to stop us selling our stuff to him."

"He might at that. Abu's not a *bad* man,

Natasha, just proud. He's only doing his job…"

"But he can't really stop us farming, can he?" I said.

"I don't know. I think he might be able to. You see, I was in town myself yesterday, talking to Joel. He's had word from the capital. Just rumours at the moment, but it seems things are hotting up there."

"Is this the coup they've been talking about?"

"Could be. They're set on this new leader."

"Someone not so fond of Brits?"

"Exactly. Sounds like no more than shouting and skirmishing at the moment, so we must hope they'll manage it all without too much bloodshed."

"But Joel's worried?"

"Joel is already planning to sell up," he said.

The thought of Joel preparing to leave his store sent a chill through me. The store meant everything to him; he'd devoted his life to building it up.

I thought Dr Pat might have a quiet word with Daddy when we got to the farm but he didn't really get the chance. Daddy more or less dragged him out of the saddle and manoeuvred him into the house to listen to a detailed account of what he intended to say when Abu next came sniffing round.

"No doubt you've got a good point,

Ronnie," Dr Pat said. "But I should be a bit careful, if I were you…"

Daddy waved his objection away and hauled him over to the dining table.

"Let's eat," he said with a fancy gesture at a tin rattling around in our largest pot. "I've opened a tin of steak and kidney pudding, saved for a special occasion. It's been steaming away for ages so it should be more or less ready."

I gave Dr Pat a questioning look – should we tell him now? – but he shook his head briefly. I understood him completely – no, not now; wouldn't do any good; might spoil his mood. It was odd how we both saw Daddy in the same way; like a boy you have to protect from the nasty secrets of the big world.

While Daddy was busy trying to lever the steaming tin out of the pot, Dr Pat leaned towards me and said in a low voice, "Ronnie's a tough old chap, my dear. Don't worry about that. He must be told, of course, but it's best if he gets used to the idea in stages. If we come straight out and tell him to leave…"

I nodded. There was no need for him to say the rest. We both knew what Daddy would do if we suggested leaving: fold his arms and stay put.

"Anyway," Dr Pat continued, "if trouble is brewing, it's brewing a long way from Mountain Farm, isn't it?"

He smiled and I smiled back, comforted somehow by his wise, plump face and the candles winking in his glasses. It never occurred to me that he might be wrong.

After the pudding and the singing – 'Ilkley Moor', several times over because Daddy insisted on it and it was the only song he could remember properly – he clapped his hands and called for silence. He stood on a stool, the top of his head brushing against the sagging roof, and I could tell he was about to make a speech. I cringed and glanced at Dr Pat, but he seemed to be enjoying it all.

"Lady and gentlemen," Daddy began, "we are gathered here to celebrate the unqualified success of Mountain Farm and our triumph over adversity and the petty interference of Abu and his ilk."

Colin gave a cheer.

"But there is something else to celebrate, too. It's a little bit early but that shouldn't stop us. Banhams never tie themselves down to dates. So, let us give a little thought to the future. To next week, in fact."

I watched a spiral of smoke from the dying fire twist through the hole in the roof and out into a grey sky. I could hear Dr Pat's horse tearing at the grass outside, and the soft murmuring of the stream beneath us.

"Next week," Daddy went on, "is Natasha's

birthday, so this is really a double celebration. And, being the thoughtful and considerate father that I am, I have prepared a little gift for her."

He reached into his shirt and pulled out a small white envelope.

"Natasha, will you step up here a moment?"

I didn't move. I was suddenly fearful – that he would embarrass me and make me feel small, that I would show my disappointment without meaning to.

"Come on, girl. I can't stand up here all night."

I stood up and walked towards him. He flourished the envelope and gave a ridiculous bow. Then the quiet of the hut was pierced by a terrified scream. It filled the house and we all froze and looked at each other.

"What was that?" said Colin.

"Not to worry, old man," Daddy said, climbing from the stool. "It's nothing."

"It's the horse, Ronnie," muttered Dr Pat. "The poor beast's taken fright at something."

Alex and I stumbled over to the door and looked out. The horse was stamping the ground, his neck arched as he pulled against a tight rope. At the other end of the rope two dark figures huddled together, shuffling their feet and trying to cling on. I saw them in silhouette against a glow of pink and grey-blue in the sky. There were rifles strapped to their backs. I jumped at the touch of Daddy's hand on my shoulder.

"What the devil do you think you're doing?" he bellowed over my head.

The figures ignored him. They were young men – I could see that now – dressed in baggy combat trousers. One had a khaki shirt open to the waist, and the dull light reflected on his chest as he strained on the rope.

"Let go of that!" shouted Daddy. "Let go at once!"

Then three more men ran by, heading for the cattle, their boots thudding on the grass and their rifles rattling. Dr Pat joined us at the door.

"What is it?" he said, quiet and bemused. "What's happening?"

We didn't answer because we didn't know what was happening. All we knew was that the place was swarming with men running here and there and taking no notice of us.

"My God, it's begun..." breathed Dr Pat.

Then one of the men detached himself from the group and walked towards us.

"Banham," he said in a ringing voice. "Do nothing foolish, Banham, and you will not be harmed."

"Abu? Is that you? What are you doing here?"

"If you don't know that," said Abu with a

smile, "then I'm afraid it's too late to explain."

I hardly recognized him. He was wearing baggy camouflage trousers and a khaki shirt. All his neatness and control had gone.

"Is this something to do with our stream?" said Daddy. "Because I can assure you…"

"Your stream, Banham? What makes you think it's yours?"

"Of course it's ours, man. I don't understand…"

"No. You never did understand. Now, if you will stand aside, we'll come in and tell you what you must do."

"Stand aside?" said Daddy. "You think I'm going to allow you into my house?"

"You really have no choice, Banham," Abu said, and he put out his hand and pushed Daddy in the chest.

He fell back a little and Abu stepped through the door. Colin was cowering behind Daddy, his eyes round and dark. He had Hubert clasped to his chest. I held out my hand to him. He ran to me, wrapping his arms round me and pressing Hubert into my ribs.

"Besides," Abu added, wandering around and looking in corners, "the house isn't yours either. Not any more."

"What are you talking about? I built this up from nothing…"

"Then that was very foolish of you. You were warned, Banham. You were told that one day you would have to leave. That day has come."

More soldiers barged in and elbowed Pat aside. He staggered and fell into a sitting position with a curse. I saw a boot raised and he crossed his arms over his head as it stamped down on his elbow. Daddy leapt to his defence, shouting, and two men had to grab his arms and hold him back. The soldier was about to kick again but Abu caught his shoulder and swung him round, staring fiercely into his face. For a long moment nobody moved. Then Abu stooped to help Pat to his feet.

"I'm sorry," he said. "My men are too keen. They have been waiting a long time for this moment."

I felt my legs trembling. They would have buckled under me if I hadn't been clinging to Colin. And everything else was trembling, too. The world was trembling. It was a heavy ball on the end of a thin thread and it was going to drop. We were going to fall. We were going to die, here in this ridiculous house with a stream running through it. If the thread breaks, I thought, if the thread breaks ... And the thread which held us was Abu. He only had to give the order, to say one word...

I looked at Daddy and tried to make him understand. *Please, Daddy, say nothing. Can't you see that Abu means what he says?* But there was no need. Daddy was completely silent, his face pale and his mouth closed tight. He looked dazed, as if all the words in the language had been knocked out of him. Alex moved beside him and took hold of his hand.

CHAPTER NINETEEN

We had no time to collect our belongings – no papers or passports, no money – but just before we were forced outside, Daddy fell to his knees and scrabbled about beneath his mattress, his fingers quick and urgent. He pulled out the wine jug and cradled it in his arms. One of the soldiers wrenched it away from him and hauled him up.

"Please," Daddy begged. "I need this ... I must take it with me…"

"You must take nothing," Abu told him. "Nothing here belongs to you."

I was too scared to think about it then, but later, when I remembered Daddy groping on the floor for the jug and pleading with the soldiers, I was appalled. His first thought was for drink. He'd become a stranger to me.

So we came away with next to nothing. Colin still had Hubert with him, and I managed to slip *War and Peace* under my shirt, but that was all. Once Daddy realized that begging for his precious jug would get him nowhere, he left Mountain Farm like someone walking in his sleep, without a backward glance. He seemed to feel nothing.

As we were walking away from our home for the last time, I looked back and saw in a patch of moonlight Colin's old pram, upended and leaning against the wall of the house.

The soldiers escorted us to Bokanna where we were put on a train to the capital. As it rattled through the darkness, Daddy sat staring out of the window in silence. A sea of blue-grey grass flickered by, broken occasionally by the silvery shape of a moonlit tree. By then I didn't care about his silence – I didn't want to talk to him – but after about an hour he suddenly turned to me and blinked.

"Pat? Where's Pat?"

"You were there," I said.

"No. I can't remember."

"He was our friend," I said, "our good friend. Didn't you even notice?"

He frowned and shook his head, so I told him. Pat had been put on his horse and sent back to his bungalow. He was a doctor – he'd be useful in the new Tumani – and anyway, he wasn't British. I'd seen him twist round in his saddle to say goodbye, his face unusually sharp in the moonlight, and I couldn't bear it.

There were two soldiers guarding us, their rifles slanted in front of us like a fence. I pushed through and ran to him.

"Leave her," Abu said. "Let her say goodbye."

I took Pat's hand and squeezed it because I didn't know what to say. He leaned down to touch me on the cheek, wiping with his thumb at tears I didn't even know I'd been crying.

"Don't worry," he said. "Just do what Abu tells you and you'll be all right."

"But what about you?"

"I'll be all right too, Natasha. When things have settled down a bit, tell Ronnie I'll miss him, won't you?"

"Oh, Pat..."

"Now, back you go, Natasha. We medical types must look after ourselves, for the sake of the others. Remember that."

He yanked on the reins and the horse circled towards the Mountain. He waved his hat and then was lost behind a wall of rock, striped with moon-shadow.

"Yes," said Daddy, looking out of the window. "I remember now."

And he fell silent again. I couldn't bring myself to give him Pat's message.

When we reached the airport, shortly after dawn, it was seething with panic. People swirled backwards and forwards, as if they'd just been dragged out of bed. Some had little cases but most, like us, had nothing. At one point, through a moving wall of shoulders, I thought I saw Joel, standing still and clutching a bundle to his chest. But someone barged into him and when he turned round I saw that he was a stranger. A stranger with wide, bewildered eyes.

We were herded into a wooden building on the edge of the airstrip. There we sat and waited – an hour, two. Then a door opened and everyone surged forward. We spilled out into the glare of the sun, and there were soldiers at the steps of a plane, counting as people shuffled past them. We edged closer to the steps and I heard someone shouting, a voice lifted above the chaos all around us. One of the soldiers had pulled Alexander out of the line and was holding him by his elbow.

"Not this boy!" he was shouting. "He cannot leave."

"Please!" I called, trying to push my way back to them. "Wait!"

It hadn't occurred to me till then that Alexander might have to stay behind and I became desperate to explain. We were four – four people from Mountain Farm – and we couldn't be separated. Four who *belonged* together. I had to tell them that, but hands and bodies kept shoving me closer to the plane. Then I heard Daddy shouting, too.

"He must come," he said, grabbing Alexander's other arm. "He's my house boy. My boy. He must come."

For a moment or two Alexander was tugged backwards and forwards between Daddy and the soldier. Voices came clamouring from the back of the line – "Keep them moving! Why have we stopped?" – until the soldier simply gave up and released his grip.

"Go on, then," he said, waving Alexander away. "Go. I don't care."

So he came with us. A thick door thudded shut, and was sealed, and he was still with us. The plane rumbled along the runway and lurched into the air.

The thread's held, I thought, and we're alive.

But when I looked across the aisle at Daddy, and saw him leaning stiffly back in his seat, with Colin's head against his shoulder and that washed-out, lost look in his eyes, I wasn't sure anymore. *Something* had broken.

I felt the plane bank and opened my eyes. It was another dawn and we were coming down over England – a countryside of brown and green squares, hedges in neat lines and tiny cars moving silently along thin roads. The weak sun flashed along roofs as we passed over them. I'd always imagined that my heart would lift when I saw England again, but all I felt was the plane tilt – and something dull and heavy inside.

We'd lost everything but I didn't care about that. Not the *things*. I minded about Pat. And my father. I felt as if I'd left them both behind. Because I didn't recognize the pathetic man sitting blankly in the seat across the aisle. The cause of all our heartache, all our loss.

The airport lounge was cold and grey. Grey light came up from the floor and huge square walls of glass let in the whitish morning. People were criss-crossing all around us, but there was no panic or jostling this time. We sat on a bench, waiting, Colin curled up with his knees under his chin and Hubert locked in his arms. Alexander was cross-legged on the floor, gazing speechlessly at all the strange things around us – loud voices coming out of the air, stairs that moved by themselves, a giant Christmas tree spangled with lights. Once we were strangers in his country, and now he was a stranger in ours. Except that it didn't really feel like our country.

A man and a woman came through the crowd towards us. They were wearing white shirts and dark ties and their heels clicked on the shiny floor.

"You must understand," they told us. "You have no money or papers so it's difficult." They were cool and polite and wanted to do things properly.

"People are always trying this," they said,

"coming up with stories… We have to check. There are rules and you can't ignore rules…"

Once this kind of talk would have riled Daddy, but now he said nothing. His elbows were on his knees and he was staring at the floor. I told them to telephone Aunt Sylvia. She would explain; she would sort it all out.

"Is that so, sir?" asked the woman, leaning down a little to catch his eye.

He turned his head and opened his mouth. But shut it again. He put his hand up to shield his eyes, and nodded.

"Can't you even speak?" I said to him.

The man and woman looked at each other and I knew they were thinking, "Trouble-maker. Who does she think she is?" But they smiled at me and I watched them head for their office to make some phone calls.

There was an odd, choked voice behind me.

"Thank you, Natasha."

"Someone had to tell them."

"Natasha, I'm sorry…"

"It's too late for that," I said. "You should've been sorry when we left the Station. You should've been sorry when you made us leave Mrs Henderson, when you almost killed Colin because of your stupid, stupid…"

He lifted his grimy face but couldn't look me in the eye. He was holding something out to me. An envelope. The envelope he'd been waving about when Abu's men had come. It was crumpled and streaked with sweat.

"What's this?" I said.

"It's for you … for your birthday…"

"After what you've done? I don't want it."

"I didn't mean it to be like this…"

I couldn't bear to look at him any longer, so I snatched the envelope from his hand and walked off, pushing through the crowds, just wanting to get away from him. I heard him calling after me – "Natasha … please…" – but I ignored him. I walked on until I came to a wall. Then I stopped and sat down, leaning against it, hugging my knees. The back of my throat tightened and my eyes and nose were running.

Banhams don't cry, he always said. They get on with life. They aren't daunted. That was his way. Well, I didn't want anything to do with Banhams anymore. I was Natasha, my mother's daughter.

After a while I felt a hand on my shoulder and shrugged it off.

"Leave me alone."

"Natash."

It was Alexander.

"Go away," I said. "Go and look after Banner Pa. I don't need you."

He knelt down beside me.

"Not be angry, Natash. He very sorry, I know…"

"He's not sorry, Alex. Only for himself.

He's the only one he cares about…"

"No. He very good to me…"

"Only because you do what he wants."

He looked stung for a moment. Then he took my wrist and held it up so I could see the envelope still crushed in my hand.

"You look, Natash," he said, gently unfolding my fingers.

He tore open the envelope, took out a sheet of lined paper, and placed it on my knees. I tried to look away but I couldn't help seeing two little pencil drawings. One was of Hubert, done by Colin, and the other a simple picture of a mountain which Daddy had probably drawn himself. Beneath them were several lines of his odd, sloping writing.

To my darling Natasha, it began. *Happy birthday. This is your present. With all my love, Daddy.*

(Now go away and read the rest by yourself.)

I remembered him standing on the stool at the party, and Pat and Colin and Alexander smiling at me and waiting to see what it was all about. But the message wasn't for them. He wanted me to read it in private. There was nothing private about a crowded airport, but I wiped my eyes with the back of my hand and read on.

I've been looking for something good enough to give my daughter, but really there isn't anything. I tried Joel's store but all I could see were saddles and buckets and brooms, and of course they won't do. So I spoke to Pat about it and got him to tell me what you'd really like. What he said surprised me, Natasha. I didn't much like it at first, but I thought about it and thought about it, and came to see that he was right. So here is your present – the best I can do.

Then there was a little sum, neatly set out and underlined. It listed the money saved from the farm over a period of three months. Totalled and converted into pounds, shillings and pence. I looked at Alexander.

"I don't understand," I said.

"He said to me, about the money, Natash. Keep for you in a jar. Look, look."

He tapped the paper with his finger and I read the rest.

There's enough here to take you back to England. I've made the arrangements and you can leave when you're ready. I'll get Sylvia to meet you off the plane. Then you can go back to school and study. We'll all miss you, but I know this is for the best and that one day you'll make us all proud. So this is to say happy birthday, and thank you, my dear, and sorry for all the trouble I've put you through. And I'm afraid I shall make rather a fool of myself when you go, so it's also to say goodbye properly.

*   *   *

He'd hardly moved. His elbows were still resting on his knees and he was studying the palms of his hands so intently that he didn't hear us approach. Someone had brought them a travel blanket and Colin was huddled inside it with only the top of his head showing. I stood there for a moment, not sure what to do or say. Alexander gave me a little push and Daddy lifted his head. There was a look of mild surprise on his face.

"I read your letter," I said, and sat down beside him.

He took a deep breath, part sigh and part shudder, then went back to examining his hands.

"There is no money, Natasha," he said. "It was in the jar and they wouldn't let me bring it."

"It doesn't matter…"

"But it does. Everything I worked for – for you and Colin – has gone. I've lost it. I had no right to do this to you. I risked all our lives. And what for? For nothing. Because in the end that's what I've done for you. Nothing."

"No," I said, taking hold of his hands. "You mustn't say that…"

Alexander gave a polite cough. He was standing proudly before us, with his arms by his side like a soldier. And smiling.

"That right, Banner Pa," he said. "You lost

199

house but you got house boy still. And now you got Natash. You not lost her."

CHAPTER TWENTY
JANUARY 1972

Word of our little steamer's progress must have gone before us up the river, so from time to time, when the trees thin out along the bank, tiny figures appear, shouting and waving at us. When they do, the guide gives me a quizzical look and I shake my head: no, not this one.

"We'll know when we get there," I tell him, "because she'll be waiting to meet us."

I'm sure she will. A straight-backed lady in a long black skirt. I long to see her again. All those years ago, when I stood at the ship's rail with Colin and looked across the bay to Liberation, I longed for something quite different – to be back in England. It was my secret but one I never managed to tell Daddy. He discovered it in the end, of course, but not until he'd dragged us halfway across West Africa with Colin's old pram.

Now I'm in Africa again, gazing out at the river bank, with my back resting against a soft leather bag and my feet propped on two crates of medical supplies for Mrs Henderson. I suppose I have a secret this time, too. And this time I won't keep it to myself. I'm going to ask Mrs Henderson if I can stay and help her. I know now that Africa is where I want to be. I feel nervous and light-headed, thinking about this question. So much has happened since last I saw her, and I can't be sure she'll want me. Still, I must ask her, and hope she'll agree. Whatever she says, I'll hand over the crates, Daddy's gift to her, and with them his good wishes.

"Give the old bat my love, Natasha," he said when I left England. "Tell her no hard feelings."

The bag I've been resting against is his special gift to me. He presented it to me on the day I graduated from medical school. A cool, sunny day in Edinburgh it was. My family around me. Aunt Sylvia and Daddy arm in arm. Colin and Alex, awkward in suits, beaming at me.

"Thank you, Daddy," I said, kissing his cheek and staring uncertainly at the bag.

"Do you like it, old girl? I made it myself."

"It's lovely. Really. What is it?"

"It's a bag, Natasha! For your medical gear."

It was his third attempt, he said proudly. Colin told me he'd lost his temper with the other two and hurled them down the bottom of Aunt Sylvia's garden. It doesn't quite sit straight, and the clasp never quite fastens properly, but it's very precious to me and I won't use anything else.

The sun is sinking fast and the steamer is ploughing through a track of shimmering gold. It's turning towards the shore where we can just make out a group of people in a little clearing.

The house is just as I remember it, like a model of an English cottage on stilts. It still stands out fresh and white against the dark green trees. And Mrs Henderson is there among her villagers. I can see her arm waving slowly above her head, and hear her voice carrying across the water.

"Welcome back, Natasha! Welcome back!"

NORMAL NESBITT,
THE ABNORMALLY AVERAGE BOY
Nick Warburton

"I am average. I am dull. I'm not surprised people can't remember my name. I'm so dull I'm afraid I might forget it myself."

Meet Gordon Nesbitt, The Average Pupil. That's what the computer says, anyway, and no one will let him forget it. In fact, to Nesbitt's increasing dismay, his normality seems to be attracting an abnormal degree of interest – even his dog gets in on the act. But when the gorgeous new girl, the Dumb Blonde, joins in, Nesbitt is moved to action – with quite extraordinary results!

"Very well done … there's much humour and many witty scenes." *Books for Keeps*

"Hilarious." *The Daily Telegraph*

TO TRUST A SOLDIER
Nick Warburton

"The rules of war, Mary. You must promise to keep them or it might be the death of us all."

Sometime in a machine-less future, six soldiers – five volunteers and a professional – are on their way to fight for their country against an invading army, when they come across a teenage girl, Mary. She becomes their map, guiding them to the battlefield – or so the men are told by their leader, the flinty, dispassionate Sergeant Talbot, whom they trust as deeply as they distrust Mary. One though, young Hobbs, feels sorry for the girl and a relationship develops between them...

"Warburton has a remarkable gift for realistic writing." *The Times*

YOU'VE BEEN NOODLED!
Nick Warburton

"Don't you see? We've been Noodled!"

Most people would take it as an insult if their teacher called them "a noodle". But not Peter Smith. He likes it so much he forms a gang called the Noodles, dedicated to behaving stupidly – much to the irritation of sensible Graham Keefe. In protest, he and his best friend Nathan form a rival gang called the Anti-Noodles – and so begin the Noodle Wars! But will it be sense or stupidity that finally wins out? All is revealed in this highly entertaining story by an award-winning author.

MORE WALKER PAPERBACKS

For You to Enjoy